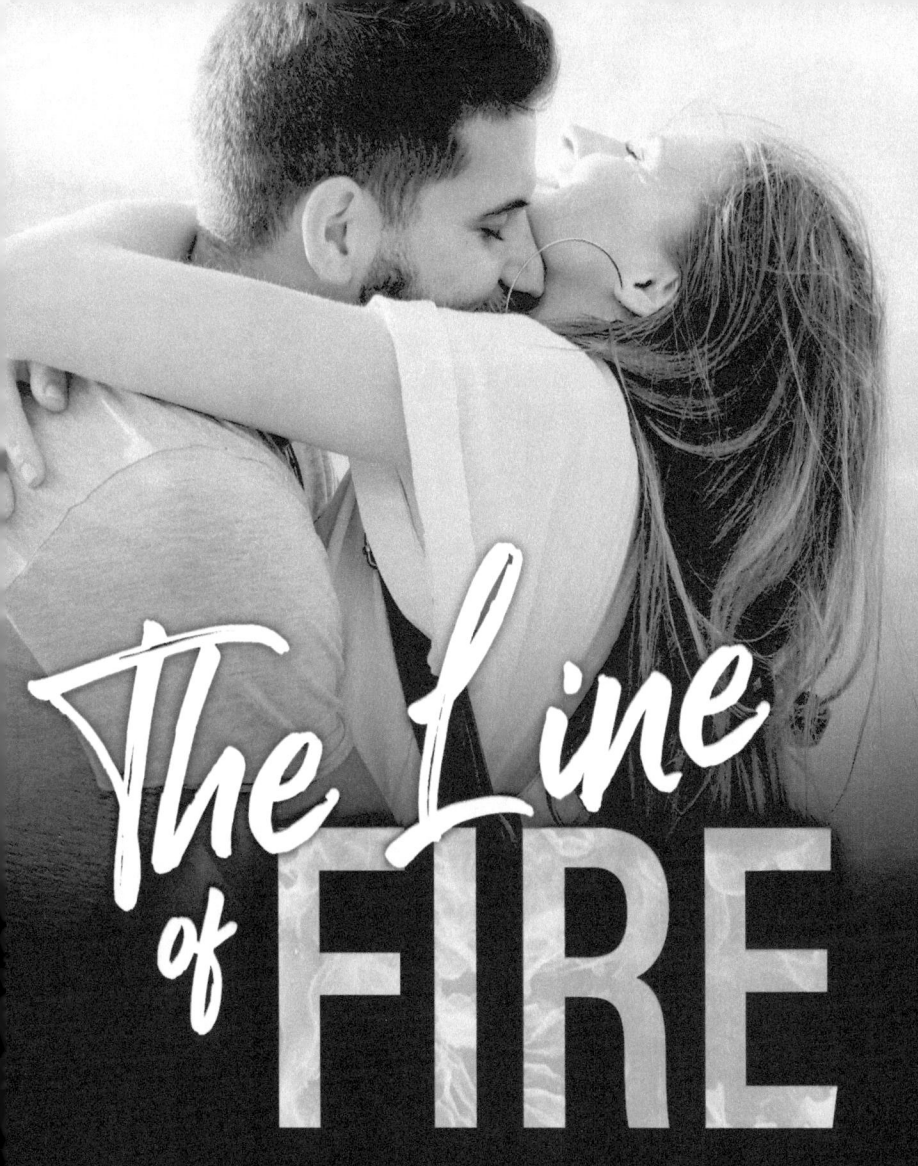

The Line of FIRE

AJ RANNEY

Rudy House Publishing

The Line of Fire

Half Moon Lake Heroes: Red Line Series Book 3

Copyright @ 2026 A.J. Ranney

Developmental & line edit by Michelle Fewer

Proofread by Hundred Proof Services

Cover by K.B. Barrett Designs

ISBN: 978-1-965124-10-9 (ebook)

ISBN: 978-1-965124-04-8 (paperback)

ISBN: 978-1-965124-19-2 (hardcover)

❀ Created with Vellum

To all those who have battled mental health.
Here's to the spirit within us that keeps us going against all odds.

Listen on Spotify!

Take My Name - Parmalee
King Of My Heart - Taylor Swift
Power Over Me - Dermot Kennedy
Mirage - Sabrina Carpenter
Only When It's You - Bleeding Verse
Forbidden Fruit - Tommee Profitt, Sam Tinnesz, brooke.
Most Beautiful Thing - Nicholas Andrea
This Is the Beginning - Ely Eira
i'm yours - Isabel LaRosa
Dangerous Woman - Ariana Grande
Burn Me Beautiful - Shadow Beloved

Chapter One

ADAM

"AND THEN HE pissed all over the tire." I chuckled, thinking back to the fiasco from earlier that week. "The look on Logan's face was priceless."

I shook my head as three kids bolted past me. It was still hard to believe the Half Moon Lake Fire Department had gone from five single guys—well six if you included Seth, who'd just joined the crew in April—to this. I looked around at all the couples and kids filling Jay and Sarah Mitchell's backyard for their daughter's third birthday party. Technically, Nora wasn't Jay's biological daughter, but he'd claimed her as his own after meeting his now wife, Nora's mother, two years ago.

"I struggled to keep a straight face when he explained it was what his parents always had him do when he needed to pee."

Sarah's eyes twinkled with humor. She was the kindergarten assistant at the school we'd visited and didn't seem at all shocked by the kid's behavior.

"Kind of surprised Logan's head didn't explode." Jay smirked. "I'm almost sad I wasn't there to witness it." He was home that day with a sick Nora, or he would have been with us laughing his ass off too. With a nod at the almost empty bottle in my hand, he asked, "Need another beer?"

"Sure."

He leaned over and pressed a kiss to Sarah's cheek. "Need anything?"

She shook her head, placing her hand on her newly obvious baby bump. Jay had been over the moon since finding out his wife was pregnant. His excitement bubbled over when he'd recently brought in ultrasound pictures to show all of us.

At nearly thirty, I never thought I'd want this life. Had always been good with casual relationships. Women I dated thought they'd be able to change me. Fix me. Make me want that. But there was nothing wrong with me. No tragic back story. I just didn't think I wanted marriage and kids.

Until recently.

Maybe it was watching all the guys around me settle down over the last two years, starting with our Lieutenant, Owen McKinley. I glanced over at where he stood with his wife Cece and their little girl, Grace. Luckily, sleeping with the chief's daughter hadn't ended in a complete clusterfuck for him.

After Owen was Jay. And then recently our driver, Logan Murray—who had an almost unhealthy obsession with our rig, but even more of an obsession with Jay's sister, Izzy—fell to the lure of family life. Izzy had gone from nanny to his twin girls to a permanent addition to their household.

I scanned the people in the backyard. Even the grumpy-ass new guy, Seth, had found someone. Only single guys left were me and Zack.

Speaking of my best friend since we were old enough to cause trouble together... Zack headed my way just as Sarah turned to talk to Jay's sister Angie and her fiancé, Wyatt. Like I said, lots and lots of couples.

Zack wrapped his arm around my neck. "Guess what I just found out?"

I sighed. Who knew what nugget of information he was going to tell me. I never understood how he was always the first one to hear shit. It was like he was a gossip and rumor magnet. "I don't know, but I'm sure you're about to tell me."

"Lyla broke up with the guy she was dating."

Oh. That. Did he think it was shocking news? The guy was an utter tool bag. Frankly, I didn't understand what took her so long to end it. "Yeah, I know."

"So what's your plan?"

"My plan?" If he was about to ask me if I was finally going to make my move, I seriously might punch him. I wasn't sure how many times I needed to tell these guys we were just friends.

"Yeah, to get your girl."

I shrugged away from him. "I've told you before we're just friends."

"Bullshit," Jay spat out as he stepped up next to me, holding out a beer. "None of us are buying that crap."

I didn't need them to believe it. Maybe when Lyla and I first met I wanted something to happen between us. But at the time, she was my student in the EMT class I was teaching. Then, as luck would have it, she was placed at our station as soon as her training was completed. She considered me a coworker and I had been officially friend zoned. Which was fine. I wasn't planning to mess that up and make things awkward at work.

It wasn't like we could avoid each other either. I had my EMT certification in addition to being a firefighter and was paired with her multiple times a month. We had to work in close quarters and together as a team. There was no way I would jeopardize that. Or our friendship, for that matter.

I crossed my arms over my chest and looked around the backyard, seeking out the girl in question. Her dark brown hair that held a strong hint of red to it fell in tight curls down her back, a striking contrast to the royal blue dress she wore. In certain lighting, especially sunlight, her hair looked almost completely red.

Zack chuckled. "Exactly." He lowered his voice before adding, "We all see how you look at her when she's not paying attention. Time to help you come up with a plan."

"Drop it," I snapped, narrowing my eyes. "I mean it, dude. Let it go."

Zack stared at me for a beat before finally crossing his arms with a pout. "Fine." The word came out like a kid who'd just been told no. "But," he added, pointing a finger in my face, "when you stop drifting down the river of denial, I have ideas for your grand gesture."

Jesus Christ. What the hell was wrong with him?

I ignored the smirk Jay still had aimed at me and pushed away from both assholes. "I'm going to get some food."

After stepping inside and grabbing a plate, I began filling it with a little bit of everything on the kitchen table.

"All this food will totally add ten pounds."

I looked up and raised a brow at Lyla as she grabbed her own plate.

"Don't start with all that crap." I pointed my fork at her, reiterating the same thing I'd told her a million times. "You look great."

I wasn't going to make things awkward by telling her that her full tits, round ass, and slight curve to her hips would make any man fall to his knees. Except for me. Because again, I was just her friend.

"It wouldn't be so bad if the weight went to my boobs, but it'll go straight to my ass."

Again, I didn't understand why that was a problem. But I didn't plan on voicing that either. We filled our plates, and I snatched an extra piece of corn bread, placing it on her plate. She had to have at least one piece.

"Ugh. You're a bad influence."

I shrugged. "You're welcome."

She rolled her eyes, but I didn't miss the slight pull of her lips as she fought a smile. "I saw you picked up the EMT shift tomorrow."

"Yup, we're working together. Are you excited?" I shot her a smirk. "We can grab food at Mamacitas between calls."

I hadn't planned on picking up a shift on my day off, but when she told me it opened up, I'd jumped at the chance. I probably wouldn't have if it were anyone else, but she was one of my favorite people to ride with and I always looked forward to working together. She was smart—knew her stuff but was also willing to learn. And she made it fun.

"And that's why you're my favorite." She popped an olive in her mouth and turned, walking back outside.

I followed her to a table where Logan and Izzy were sitting. His twin daughters were still running around the yard somewhere. Lyla took the seat next to Izzy and the two started chatting. Lyla had originally become friends with Izzy over a year ago when their mutual friend Nicole had introduced Izzy to her group of friends.

I sat across from Logan, smiling as I listened to Lyla rave about Izzy's ring. "Congratulations, man."

We all knew he was going to pop the question last night. I wasn't so sure how all that was going to turn out back in May, especially since Logan didn't want to take my advice and talk to Jay before anything happened with his sister, but it all worked out in the end.

"Thanks." Logan's lips lifted into a wide smile. It was good to see him so happy and smiling so much lately. It was obvious Izzy brought that out in him.

The rest of our crew began filling chairs at the long table. Multiple conversations were happening at once, and I sat back, taking it all in with a smile. We might be a loud, chaotic bunch, but I loved it. We felt more like family than anything else. Something I wished I'd had growing up. It was just my mom, me, and my sister, so now that our crew had grown, incorporating women and kids, I finally felt like part of a big family.

Lyla laughed and it drew my attention to her. She caught my eye and raised a brow. I sent her a wink and she rolled her eyes. This was the dynamic we had. I could openly flirt with her, and she would brush it off with a roll of her eyes or a shake of her head. Because we were just friends. Nothing more.

After everyone finished eating, we sang happy birthday to Nora and had cake. The party began winding down, and people started to leave. Families with smaller kids were the first to clear out, their kids either exhausted from running around or hitting a major sugar crash. I was just about to head out when Lyla stepped back into the yard. She'd said she was leaving a bit ago, so why was she back out here?

"I need a jump," she announced.

Standing across from me, Zack hid a smirk behind the lip of his beer bottle just as Logan leaned over close to me. "Better go help your girl."

"She's not—" Why was I even bothering? "Jesus, never mind." I pushed away from the group and headed toward Lyla. "Come on, I got ya."

She turned, walking back around the side of the house. "It's been one thing after another this week. Like ending things with Ted wasn't enough, I've been puked on, lost one of my favorite earrings, and now this."

Her ramblings jarred my memory. "Oh, I found it."

She spun without warning, and I collided into her with an *oof*, almost toppling us both to the ground. My hands braced against her lower back, keeping her upright, while I found my footing. Most of the time her clumsiness was endearing. Other times, I was just glad to have quick reflexes.

With her hands flat against my chest, she glanced up at me, blue irises shining bright, pulling me in. Long lashes framed her eyes and freckles dusted her fair skin. A loose curl fell in front of her face, and I fought every urge to brush it back. Ensuring she was stable on her feet, I stepped back quickly, before she could feel my reaction to having her in my arms.

Dammit. I'd been so good about controlling my physical reaction to her. But that was twice in the last week I'd failed. Maybe her having a boyfriend had helped me put her in the completely off-limits just-friends category. I needed to figure out how to get back there now that she was single again. Because the last thing I needed was for her to figure out I actually found her attractive. That would ruin everything, I was sure of it.

"Sorry," she mumbled. "You found my earring?"

I nodded. "Yeah. I went back this morning and found it. It was a lot easier to spot in the daylight."

I'd meant to give it to her when I got here, but totally forgot and left it in the car. Before I realized what she was doing, she closed the distance between us and wrapped her arms around my neck.

"Thank you." Her warm breath skated across my skin.

Fucking hell.

My mom. My sister. Baseball. Snakes. I continued to think of five more things that I found undesirable.

My shoulders finally relaxed after she stepped back and turned, moving forward again. I stared after her, hoping that was the last incident of having her pressed against my body. At least until I could figure out how to stop my dick from reacting to her touch.

Maybe taking that shift with her tomorrow wasn't the best move. But working together wouldn't involve touching. It'd be fine.

And it would be the perfect way to place her firmly back into the coworker and friend category. My plan was foolproof.

Chapter Two

LYLA

"Do you think it's the arsonist?" I shifted nervously in the passenger seat as Adam drove the ambulance to the location of the fire. Not the best way to start a shift.

Early morning, hours before the sun had fully risen, a vacant building, and with it being the beginning of October, meant it could be our serial arsonist. Whoever it was had been causing havoc in Half Moon Lake since the beginning of the year. It was unusual for something like this to happen in a small, quiet town. Even though I hadn't grown up here, my hometown forty minutes away was similar. Just like ours, you would find an occasional drunk driver or bar fight, but a serial arsonist? Highly unlikely.

"Definitely possible. Has his MO written all over it." His

hands tightened on the steering wheel as he confirmed what I was thinking.

Regardless of where we were headed, I was super excited that Adam had picked up this shift. There were only a handful of people I enjoyed riding with. Some of the paramedics and older EMTs treated me with kid gloves, not really giving me a chance to learn and grow. I was a hands-on learner, and fortunately, Adam understood that and gave me the chance to apply the things he'd taught me. He seemed to recognize that if I needed help, I wouldn't hesitate to say so.

One of the paramedics, Kyle Williams, was good about that too. He used to be an army medic until he was medically discharged. He had some truly interesting, but also heartbreaking stories to tell. But most of all, I loved hearing about his wife and kids. He lit up every time he talked about them. There were a few others I liked working with, but overall, Adam was my favorite.

It helped that we were friends. We liked the same music—mostly country—and had the same taste in food. Conversation between us came easily. He listened and didn't judge. Even when I complained about my ex, Ted.

My best friend Mia was always quick to roll her eyes, telling me to dump his stupid ass every opportunity she got. She rarely sugarcoated anything, and was thoroughly delighted when Ted and I finally called it quits after four months. And even though I knew Adam agreed, he let me vent and process, never throwing it back in my face. I appreciated that.

This would be my third arson fire since I'd joined the Half Moon Lake fire department as an EMT in July. Seth's girlfriend Violet was the crime scene tech assisting with the case, and they still had no hard evidence or new leads. They'd had a suspect back in May, but weren't able to prove he was responsible, leaving everyone frustrated and the police department back to square one.

"You good?" Adam's voice broke through my endless thoughts.

I looked over at him, his concern etched in every feature, and nodded. "Yeah, I'm good. It's just nerve-racking." Every time we got called to one of these fires, I worried that this would be the one where someone got severely injured, or worse. But I also didn't want to voice that thought out loud. Call me superstitious, but I liked to keep my worst-case scenarios in my head. Putting them out there made me feel like it might call it into existence.

He parked the ambo in a safe spot away from the fire and turned toward me, reaching out and gripping my shoulder. "I know. But so far, we haven't had any injuries or casualties."

I worried my bottom lip between my teeth. "True. But each time there's always a chance. And what if he sets a vacant building on fire with a squatter inside?"

I cringed at the thought. Our small town had a low homeless population, and very few of them took to occupying vacant buildings in the area. But it was still a possibility.

"Let's not go there. If you stress and worry about every possible outcome with this job, it'll eat away at you." He studied me for another moment, then, with a reassuring squeeze of my shoulder, he opened the door and climbed out.

While he made his way over to check in with the second shift lieutenant, who was acting incident commander, I made my way around to the back of the ambo to prep the supplies that might be needed for possible injuries. After making sure everything was ready, I jumped out of the back and cursed my clumsiness as I teetered on my feet before gaining my balance. I was always on high alert and constantly taking in my surroundings when working—especially at a fire scene—so I wasn't surprised when movement on the edge of my peripheral vision caught my attention, and I turned to look that way.

The sun hadn't completely risen, so everything was cast in shadows, but I could still make out a figure standing near the tree line a couple hundred feet away. I took a few steps that way and froze as the man glanced my way before quickly turning and sprinting into the woods. It was hard to make out the color, but he was definitely wearing a dark sweatshirt with the hood up.

My body went rigid and unease crept in. The arson suspect the police had on camera, someone who'd followed Violet around in a grocery store, wore a dark green hoodie. Could the man I just saw be our arsonist?

A hand landed on my shoulder, and I jumped with a muffled shriek, spinning around to see Adam standing there with a mix of confusion and concern marring his features.

"What's wrong?" he asked.

I took in a steadying breath and glanced back over my shoulder. "I saw someone."

He cocked a brow. "You saw someone?"

"Yeah." Based on his expression, he probably thought I was talking nonsense. But I know what I saw. "Like a figure lurking near the trees. They were wearing a dark hoodie."

His eyes widened. "A green hoodie?"

"I couldn't tell." I crossed my arms, rubbing my hands up and down my upper arms. "Might've been."

He stepped forward and gripped my shoulders, glancing back toward the tree line. "I'll call Dylan and give him a heads up."

I pulled my bottom lip between my teeth. "We don't even know if the fire is arson yet."

"Yeah, but this way Dylan can make the call if he wants to head over yet or not."

I sighed when Adam pulled me into him, melting into his arms, feeling safe. It was only for a few seconds, and although I wasn't ready for my bubble of safety to burst, he was stepping back and fishing his phone out to call Dylan.

Was I being ridiculous? Plenty of people gathered near fires to watch. It was basic human nature to be curious. Plus, plenty of men wore dark colored hoodies. And we weren't even sure the fire was set on purpose.

But why was he all the way over near the tree line and not near the street, the place most lookie-loos gathered?

I was likely overreacting. Wouldn't be the first time. I was constantly being told I was too eager to push the panic button.

And although I didn't agree with the term, I could admit I tended to worry and jump to worst-case scenarios. But it wasn't always in every situation, and truthfully, when I did, my gut was usually right.

And right now, my gut was saying the figure I saw was the serial arsonist.

Chapter Three

LYLA

I SMILED behind the lip of my beer bottle as Izzy recounted the whole proposal to Nicole and Mia. I had heard some of this already at the birthday party on Saturday, and we'd already gotten some details through text, but since we were meeting up for dinner and drinks, it became the opportune time to fill us all in on all the details.

"I really thought the girls were making a picture with the chalk and they didn't want me to see it until they were done." She chuckled. "I was so surprised when I came out and they stepped aside to reveal the message just as Logan dropped to one knee."

"That's adorable." Nicole lifted Izzy's hand, looking at the ring again. "And the ring is so gorgeous."

"He definitely has good taste in jewelry," Mia added with a smirk.

That was probably as much as we were going to get from Mia on this topic. If her friends were happy, she was good with that. But when it came to talk of love and commitment, sometimes I thought she would crawl out of her skin. She'd had a rough childhood and not a lot of positive examples of solid relationships. Her mom was always looking for Prince Charming, but none of the guys she dated ever stuck around. I think it really did a number on Mia. At least in the way she viewed men. Sometimes I wondered if her job as a 911 dispatcher was perfect for her or if it just fed into her tendency to always think the worst of people.

We talked a bit more, learning Izzy wanted a spring wedding and a coed bachelor and bachelorette party. I wasn't sure exactly what my role would be, but I was excited for it all.

Mia nudged my arm, gaining my attention. "Now that you're single again... There's some hot guy at the bar looking at you."

I shook my head. The idea of jumping right back into dating someone was absolutely not on my radar. I was too clumsy, too curvy, too dramatic, too everything for Ted. He didn't always say those exact things, but his subtle criticisms slowly crept into everything, definitely making me feel them. I had no interest in dealing with that crap again. Single again at twenty-seven, I had to wonder if I would ever find someone to settle down with.

"Or your hot firefighter." Mia tipped her chin over my shoulder.

I looked behind me at the guys coming in the door. It was my day off, and I spent time with my parents on their farm, then came out with the girls. But Adam and the rest of the crew were on shift today.

"Friends with benefits is always fun."

"Don't start that again, Mia." I narrowed my eyes at her.

She shrugged. "What? A little no-strings-attached sex with a friend? What's wrong with that?"

Izzy choked on her drink as Nicole chuckled. I rolled my eyes.

This wasn't the first time Mia had brought this up, and each time I would explain we weren't like that. We were just friends. I had tried a little subtle flirting in those weeks when he was my instructor, and there wasn't a single inkling that he was interested. And now that we were friends and coworkers, I liked what we had. Even if he would be down for a friends with benefits situation, there was no way I would go there and risk messing up our personal and professional relationship.

I opened my mouth to respond, but snapped it shut as I sensed someone sidle up on the other side of me. Adam reached over and stole a few fries from my plate, popping them in his mouth with a smirk while Logan made his way around the high top to where Izzy sat.

I pushed my plate closer to Adam. "You can have them."

He raised a brow, took a few more, and then pushed the plate back in front of me. "You've barely touched them, and I happen to know they're your favorite."

I sighed. He wasn't wrong. But between the bun on the burger I had and the second beer I'd been nursing, I didn't need any more carbs.

Izzy turned to Nicole and Mia. "Do you guys care if the boys join us?"

Zack didn't wait for their response, already pulling up a stool at the end of the table between Nicole and Mia, shooting them both his signature smile. Mia glared back and huffed before looking over at me.

"Did they have to bring the annoying one?"

Working with these guys since July, I'd come to enjoy Zack's carefree, happy-go-lucky personality. It was refreshing. But I'd also quickly realized he wasn't everyone's cup of tea.

I shrugged and glanced around. "Where's Jay and Owen?"

"They went home to their wives and kids," Adam answered.

That tracked. "What about Seth?"

"You think he would choose to come out with us to a bar over going to Violet's?"

"Right." I chuckled. "Forget I asked that."

Adam pulled up a stool next to me and Logan did the same on the other side next to Izzy. He leaned in and pressed his lips to her cheek. I smiled. He was so crazy about her and it showed in everything he did. One day, maybe I'd find someone who looked at me like that.

Zack reached over and attempted to grab a fry from Mia's plate, but she pulled it away. "Get your own fries."

"Lyla shared hers. How come you won't share?" He sent her a dramatic pout. "You know, sharing is caring."

I stifled a laugh as he tried grabbing another fry and she slapped his hand away.

"Ugh. You're the worst," she huffed.

"Don't you share a bedroom with Lyla? Seems like sharing a single fry with me wouldn't be that hard." He propped his elbow on the table and rested his chin on his hand. "Inquiring minds want to know, do you two sleep in the same bed?"

She rolled her eyes. "You must have been dropped on your head as a baby."

He was really trying his best to rile her up tonight. Maybe our living situation was...different, but it worked out well for us. I had been living with my parents since quitting my boring desk job in a real estate office last year, taking some time to figure out what I really wanted to do. After I finished my EMT training, I got assigned to Half Moon Lake, and I really wanted to be closer to the station. My parents' farm was two towns over and a forty-minute commute.

It was doable, but when Izzy decided to move in with Logan, she'd asked me if I was interested in taking over her apartment. Mia was also looking for something since her lease was just about up, and she wasn't interested in renewing it. We'd talked about maybe finding something together, and the only thing that had come available in Half Moon Lake was Izzy's apartment. It was just a one-bedroom, but we decided to make it work. We could do it for the remainder of the lease and then try to find a two-bedroom after that.

Adam leaned close and whispered, "Will those two ever get along?"

I shook my head. "I wouldn't count on it." They were like oil and water, and as long as Zack took every chance he had to torment Mia, she would continue to find him annoying.

"I wonder which one of you will be the next victim of the love curse." Zack glanced over at me and then back at Mia with a smile.

Adam and I groaned in unison. He thought the whole thing was as dumb as I did, but supposedly the last four tenants had found love while living in the apartment. Adam and Zack had joked about it being cursed. And surprisingly, Mia had been reluctant about living there when I told her. I just assumed she'd laugh it off like I did, but even the slightest chance of being bitten by the love bug was enough to make her hesitate.

"Totally Lyla. I don't do love."

"Too much sharing, huh?"

She threw her hands up in the air. "Oh my God, if I give you some of my fries will you sit there and be quiet?"

His smile grew and he nodded as he pretended to zip his lips. "Not a sound."

"Great." She pushed her plate violently toward him.

He stopped the plate before it slid off the table, and with a victorious grin, he popped a fry into his mouth.

I stole a glance over at Adam, who sat there shaking his head at the exchange.

"How was shift?" I asked.

Adam shrugged. "We saved a bunch of kittens from a storm drain."

"Isn't that more animal control's job?"

"That's exactly what I said." Logan huffed. "But they needed us to help get the grate off."

"Ah. Makes sense."

We listened as they explained how the call went. None of us were surprised that Zack was filmed holding one of the kittens, and apparently, the video had already been posted on social media.

"It already has a couple hundred likes." Zack's smile widened even more. Unlike most of the crew, he loved the limelight and rarely missed an opportunity to be in it. "Maybe it'll go viral and I'll have single women lining up to bring me baked goods. I love me some chocolate chip cookies, or brownies, or really anything sweet." He sent Mia a wink. "Sour can be yummy too, though."

"Ew, gross." Mia huffed and rolled her eyes. "You're disgusting."

I couldn't hold back the chuckle that slipped out. Like I said, I was used to Zack's goofy personality and it didn't surprise me at all that he enjoyed the attention. Seth had hated the spotlight and the dozens of trays of baked goods he received for his viral video, but of course Zack gave him shit about it. In Zack's mind, attention and yummy sweets equaled greatness.

After another moment, we all fell into easy conversation. As I looked around the table, even with a few of the guys missing, it made me happy how well our small group meshed.

Well, except for Mia and Zack. But maybe eventually they would grow to like each other.

Chapter Four

ADAM

I WAVED the traffic past the firehouse as Logan finished backing the rig through the bay doors. We'd just arrived back at the station after a call to a local apartment building. Teenagers had triggered an alarm by smoking in the stairwell. I rolled my eyes thinking about the damn kids. But I was also happy it wasn't anything major.

Walking up next to the passenger side of the truck, I removed my jacket, hanging it from one of the yellow poles that separated the two bays. My suspenders, turnout pants, and boots followed suit, setting them back up and slipping back into my station boots. I followed the guys up the steps, glancing back over my shoulder as Seth walked in the opposite direction toward his girlfriend Violet, who'd just stepped inside.

I wasn't sure what I wanted to do first, relax back in one of the recliners or make a cup of coffee. I decided on the latter. A hot cup of coffee sounded great. I went through the motion of setting up a pod and brewing a cup, adding cream and sugar to it once it was finished.

I picked up the mug and froze halfway to my lips as the radio on the table behind me crackled and the voice of Kyle Williams, one of our paramedics, came through. My stomach dropped as he advised dispatch his ambo had been involved in a wreck and he was requesting an ambulance for his partner.

Unconscious.

Bleeding.

It felt like I was hearing his words in slow motion.

Because Lyla was riding with him today.

No. This wasn't happening.

Not Lyla.

I forced the shock away and spun, heading toward the stairs.

"Ricktor," Owen's voice barely registered through my subconscious as he shouted my last name.

I didn't have time to explain to him or ask him if we could load up. Lyla was only a few miles away. We would probably make it to the scene long before another ambulance would. At least then I could help get her stable. Because there was no way she wasn't going to be okay.

Her laugh filtered through my head. How she would light up with a smile whenever I agreed to Mexican food. Because she loved nachos. And tacos.

How she would trip over her own two feet and just shrug it off.

It felt like I couldn't descend the stairs quick enough, and that we were all moving in slow motion as we climbed in the truck. Honestly, I wasn't even sure I heard anything anyone was saying.

A hand landed on my shoulder, and I glanced back as Logan pulled the rig out onto the street.

30

"She's gonna be okay." Zack's slight smile did nothing to ease my worry.

I just needed to get there. To get eyes on her and see for myself that she was okay.

I held back a scream of frustration as Logan slowed the rig when we approached a red light. The lights and sirens were already on, but he blew the horn as we approached, making sure the intersection was clear before speeding up once more.

Jesus. The scene came into view—the ambulance half up on a curb, tipped onto its side— and I took a deep pull of air through my nose. I wasn't going to be of any help to her if I didn't have my head on straight.

She was a victim of a bad accident.

Not my friend.

Not Lyla.

I jumped out and headed toward the rear of the ambulance, catching sight of Kyle climbing out of the back. One eyebrow raised as he took in me and the rest of the crew behind me.

"Figured we'd get here first and help," I explained.

Kyle held his wrist against his body and gave me a brief nod.

"What happened?" All I wanted to do was get to Lyla, but I needed to stay professional, assess the full situation. I couldn't just go off half-cocked. There was a process to this, and the more information we knew the better we could do our jobs and get everyone out safely. But the sight of the ambo laying on its side sat like lead in my gut and screamed at me to do something.

"Someone ran us off the road."

His tone had the hairs on my arms standing up, and I glanced around. Not another vehicle stopped nearby. But that conversation could wait.

"You okay?" Seth asked Kyle, probably noticing the same thing I did.

"Yeah, I think it's just a sprain. Help me get them stabilized. I didn't want to risk moving them by myself."

I nodded and stepped into the back of the ambulance,

wanting nothing more than to go straight to Lyla, but knowing I'd have more room to work if we got the older man out first. "Need to move the stretcher out first."

We worked quickly to carry the patient out on the gurney. As Seth and Kyle began assessing him for further injuries, I turned back, kneeling by Lyla's side.

She groaned, opening her eyes and looking at me. Some of the tension I'd been holding drained away as relief flooded me.

Thank God.

"Kyle?" she mumbled, her eyebrows pulled together as she searched my face.

Shit. Confusion. Definitely a concussion. "Shh. Don't move." I used my hands to assess and feel for bleeding and injuries. She also had a dislocated right shoulder—I could see that easily—but couldn't tell if anything was torn or broken. The cut near her right temple, close to her hairline, looked superficial, but it would probably need a few stitches.

"What do you need?" Jay asked, climbing in behind me.

Lyla flinched and howled in pain as I ran my hands over her right side.

Fuck. That wasn't good. Bruised ribs for sure. Hopefully none were broken.

"Need a neck brace and a sling for her arm," I said as I finished my assessment. Her breathing was fine, but the fact that she just lost consciousness again worried me.

I took the brace from Jay and placed it around her neck, then cradled her arm in the sling, securing it snugly across her chest.

I glanced back at Jay. "Alcohol pad and bandage."

She hissed as I cleaned the cut. I couldn't help but smile. Sensing pain was a good thing. She was going to be fine.

Kyle appeared at the open door. "First transport is here. Who are we sending?"

I gritted my teeth, hating that I couldn't say Lyla. But the older man with cardiac and breathing issues was priority. "The patient."

I finished bandaging her cut and then examined her for any other obvious injuries. Looked as if her right side took the brunt of the impact.

When the next ambulance pulled up, I climbed to the other side of Lyla. With Jay's help, we carried her out and placed her on the stretcher. I ran down her injuries and what I'd already done with the responding EMTs, and they went through their own quick assessment before loading her up.

I glanced around the scene, seeking out Owen. Our eyes locked and I braced for a fight.

"I'm going with her," I called, waiting for his argument. Not that I had any intention of backing down.

His eyes widened slightly before he relaxed and nodded.

"Here," Kyle hollered, jogging toward me with her bag.

I nodded and took it from him, turning and heading toward the ambulance.

My priority was making sure Lyla was okay, but then I wanted to find out what the fuck had happened. Someone caused this and then left the scene. Why?

The questions sat heavy in my gut as we drove toward the hospital.

Chapter Five

LYLA

EVERYTHING FELT FUZZY, like waking up from a deep sleep. A steady beeping broke through the haze, and I tried opening my eyes, only to squeeze them shut again as my head throbbed. I shifted slightly and winced when pain radiated through my shoulder and down my side.

I breathed deep, the smell of antiseptic and bleach invading my senses. Ever so slowly this time, I pried one eye open and then the other.

White, sterile walls. A heart rate monitor and an IV bag hung off to one side.

I was in a hospital room. But why? What happened? The last thing I could recall was being in the back of the ambulance taking the blood pressure of an older patient who'd had a heart attack.

I glanced down my body. My right arm was in a sling, but other than that, I saw no additional signs of injuries. I wiggled my fingers and toes, then went through checking for feeling in all my extremities. My breathing and heart rate seemed normal as well. My left wrist had a hospital band wrapped around it with my name, Lyla Freeman, my birthday, and today's date on it.

A head of dark hair rested on muscular forearms on the side of my bed. The noticeable and detailed ink covering most of the skin below the elbows was another sure giveaway if I didn't already know who it was.

Adam.

I opened my mouth to say his name, but instead, a sound more like a croak came out.

He lifted his head and searched my face. Relief, and something else I couldn't discern, swam in his irises.

I cleared my throat. "What happened?" This time my voice stayed steady but it had a slight rasp to it.

His brows pulled together slightly. "What do you remember?"

"Nothing. Just being in the back with a patient."

His large hand covered mine. "You guys were in an accident."

I figured as much. "How? Kyle alright? The patient?"

He nodded. "Kyle's fine. Walked away with just a sprained wrist. So is the patient." With a visible breath, he studied me, indecision warring in his eyes. "Kyle said a car ran him off the road and then took off."

"Like on purpose?" I tilted my head and winced, reminding myself not to move too suddenly, or too much.

"From what I understand, yes."

"Why would someone do that?"

Adam opened his mouth to respond, but another male voice cut him off.

"Because the arsonist thinks you can ID him."

We both glanced toward the open door where Dylan stood.

"What?" My mouth fell open. The arsonist ran us off the

road? I started to shake my head, but then thought better of that sudden movement. "But I can't."

"I'm aware." Dylan sighed. "But he doesn't know you didn't get a good look."

Adam sat back in his chair, folding his large forearms across his chest. "Have you figured out who it is?"

"No. We went to question the Taylor kid and his mom said he was away visiting friends."

"And you believe her?"

"Nope. Too convenient. But she's not giving us anything either, so right now he's in the wind. And we're still trying to track down the kid's godfather to question him."

When I first started at the station, Adam had filled me in about what they knew so far about the Taylors. The son was originally considered a suspect after a matchbook at one of the scenes had led the police to the family. Evidently, the father had been pulled from a fire seven years ago and died a year later. But they couldn't determine a motive and hadn't been able to prove the kid was involved in any of the recent arsons. It was later determined that the fire where they found the matches wasn't the work of the arsonist either, sending everyone back to square one.

Their research on the family did result in turning up a godfather who was a retired firefighter. They started looking at him as a suspect in the arson cases because he had knowledge that would be useful to someone starting fires, but they still had no solid evidence to arrest either suspect.

Dylan's expression hardened as he turned my way. "Which brings me to why I'm here. I don't want you staying alone right now."

"She's staying with me."

Adam spoke quickly, and forgetting about not making any sudden movements, I whipped my head toward him and winced. "I am?"

"Yes. Even without this new development, Doc says you

shouldn't be alone for at least the first week, if not longer, depending on how long your concussion lingers. Figured you'd prefer my place over staying with your parents." He raised a brow, challenging me to disagree.

Which I couldn't. He and I both knew my mom would smother me and drive me insane.

"Don't you have a job?" Dylan narrowed his eyes at Adam. "Her parents might be a better idea."

"I have so much time accrued, I can take at least the first week off. A few days each week after that if needed as well." Adam turned and looked at me. "The girls and your parents offered to help on the days I have to work. Although your mom does want to try to convince you to stay with them."

I looked around the room. Was anyone else here?

As if Adam could read my mind, he answered my internal question. "Izzy had to go pick up the girls from school and Nicole had to head back to work. Mia and your parents are downstairs grabbing food."

"I can make sure patrol keeps an eye on your place on the days you have to work," Dylan offered.

Did I get a say in any of this?

Like he was in my head again, Adam squeezed my hand and said, "But ultimately, it's your call."

I really didn't want to stay with my parents. My mom worried about everything all the time and would make a fuss over me constantly. I didn't want that. Mia worked weird hours as a dispatcher, so staying in our apartment probably wouldn't work if I couldn't be alone. Given the way my head felt, I was sure I had a pretty bad concussion. So, aside from the possible threat that might be lurking out there, I knew I shouldn't be alone for the first week anyway. Adam knew what to watch out for and how to handle any issues that might arise.

I sighed. Adam was right in his assumptions. I'd prefer to stay with him over my parents. And honestly, I didn't want to lead the arsonist to my parents' farm either. It was secluded—just like some of the other farmhouses he had already set on fire.

Somehow, Adam's apartment felt safer. And surely he wouldn't hover and fuss over me like my mother would. He was just doing a favor for a friend.

Right?

Chapter Six

ADAM

I OPENED the door to my apartment and stepped inside, holding it open for Lyla. I saw the surprise in her parents' faces when I'd offered up my place for Lyla to stay while she recovered. Knew there was likely some disappointment on their part, too. That they would see her "choosing" me over them as a bit of a slight. But I knew it was the right choice. I knew Lyla. She was independent, and on more than one occasion had complained about how her mom worried about everything under the sun—especially when it came to Lyla's career choice. I didn't think she'd be happy staying with them.

I placed a hand on the small of her back and led her to one of my oversized armchairs. "Want me to make tacos tonight?"

She smiled up at me. "Oh, I'd die for your tacos."

I flinched. I never wanted to hear her say "I" and "die" in the same sentence ever again.

"What's wrong?" Her brows pulled together as she stared at me.

"Nothing." I shook my head then walked toward the back of the apartment to deposit her duffel on the bed in the spare room. I'd helped her pack it when we stopped by her apartment before coming here.

That was fun. She collected all her clothes and put me in charge of fitting everything in the bag. I almost completely lost it when she placed a bunch of bras and panties on her bed for me to pack. Like she didn't bat an eye. But of course she didn't. She saw me as just a friend, not a guy who would imagine her wearing said undergarments. Regardless, there was no way I could touch them, so I did the most logical thing—I draped a T-shirt over them, wrapping it around them, and put the whole bundle in the bag.

I took a quick glance around the guest room. I'd barely used it since Zack got his own place last year, and mostly only when my sister came to visit. She preferred staying with me rather than with our mom. She and Mom rarely saw eye to eye. Janet wanted freedom, and my mom didn't care that she was twenty-four, she still had rules. So, more often than not, Janet crashed with me.

I did a double check, making sure the room was good to go. The bed was made, dresser and nightstand clutter free. I pulled a few extra pillows from the closet so she could prop herself up if she needed to, and then made my way back to Lyla.

I found her in the kitchen, standing in front of the fridge with the door open.

"What are you doing?" I asked.

"Getting something to drink."

I took the jug of orange juice from her hands and placed it on the counter. "Stubborn woman," I mumbled, leading her back out of the kitchen. "You need to rest and let me take care of you."

She spun toward me with her left hand on her hip and a glare trained on me. "I didn't want to stay with my parents because I

THE LINE OF FIRE

didn't want them fussing over me. Don't tell me you're going to do the same thing now."

I lifted my hands up in mock surrender. "Easy now." Her pupils flared and I bit back a smirk. "Not trying to fuss, but, no offense, you're a bit clumsy when you *don't* have a concussion and a bad arm. I'm just trying to avoid cleaning up a mess."

If I was Pinocchio, my nose would have grown a whole foot. Because honestly, I really did want to take care of her.

With a roll of her eyes, she reached out and swatted my stomach with the back of her hand. I fought the urge to catch her wrist and pull her against me. I'd been fighting the urge to hold her since the moment she woke up in the hospital. Maybe even before that.

I searched her face and let out a sigh. "Look, just give me a few days. Rest and let me help you. Once I'm sure you're not going to get dizzy or lose your balance, I promise I'll stop fussing."

As if my words sunk into her subconscious, she reached out, gripping my arm and pinched her eyes shut. "I think you're right."

Shit. I laced my arm around her back and led her back to the chair, attempting to push the worry away. I knew what to expect. What to watch for. This was normal, and exactly what I thought might happen if she tried to do too much too fast. But reminding myself of all that was easier said than done.

I studied her for a moment, until she squinted one eye open to look up at me.

"I'm okay," she offered. "Now that I'm stable, can I have that glass of orange juice?"

"Of course." I headed back to the kitchen and poured her a cup, bringing it to her a minute later. "Here ya go."

She opened her eyes and smiled at me. "Thank you."

I nodded, attempting to push away the sensation that raced through me from her smile. "You're welcome. I'm going to start the tacos. Just holler if you need anything."

"Okay."

As I prepared the meal, I couldn't help but peek back in on her. It sucked that I didn't have an open concept apartment. I wanted to be able to see her as I cooked. Talk to her. Was she bored? Watching TV was out of the question for at least the first few days. But she seemed to be resting and content, so I went back to prepping all the ingredients for the tacos.

Once I was ready to plate everything, I stepped back into the living room. "Did you want to try to eat at the table?" I hooked a thumb behind me toward the small dining area outside the kitchen. "Or in here?"

She slowly sat up straight. "Table would be nice."

I offered her my hand, and when her fingers brushed against mine, a buzz of electricity shot up my arm and through my body. As I led her to one of the chairs, I couldn't help but wonder if she felt it too.

"Want more orange juice?"

She scrunched her nose as she looked up at me. "With tacos?"

I shrugged. I'd seen her have weirder combinations, like pizza and milk. The first time I witnessed that, I truly thought something was wrong with her.

"Gross." She shook her head. "Water is fine."

I chuckled softly as I walked back into the kitchen, grabbing us both waters and bringing them back to the table. "You want yours like you usually have them?"

"Yes. Please. Extra—"

"Guacamole," I finished for her. Months of eating at Mamacitas and a few nights of making us tacos here while we watched a movie had her preferences when it came to this dish etched in my brain.

She nodded and smiled. I stared at her for probably longer than I should have, remembering the moment in the truck as we drove toward the accident and I thought about her smile, her laugh. I turned back to the kitchen, shaking off the memory as I plated our food.

I brought our plates to the table and sat down across from her. "Your mom coming over tomorrow?"

"Yeah. She's going to help me shower and wash my hair."

I willed my brain not to think of Lyla naked and soapy. Friends didn't do that. "I'll probably run to the grocery store while she's here. Just let me know what you want, and I'll get it."

She nodded. "Okay. Thanks."

"I'll need to let Dylan know so he can have patrol drive by while I'm gone."

A sigh passed through her lips. "I really think he's wrong about this whole thing."

I cocked a brow. "Wrong about what?"

"The arsonist coming after me." She shrugged. "It could have just been an accident. People flee the scene for so many different reasons. Wouldn't be the first time we've seen that at a crash site."

"Getting scared and fleeing the scene of an unintentional collision, sure. But Kyle was pretty adamant the car purposely ran him off the road." I studied her before adding, "And he used to be military. Personally, I trust his instincts."

"I do too. But, I don't know... Assuming it was the arsonist because he *thinks* I can ID him seems like a pretty big stretch."

"I don't think it's that much of a stretch at all." It was suspicious enough that they hadn't been able to locate the kid. But then Dylan had updated us earlier that the godfather finally turned up back at his house with a gash on his left cheek. One consistent with an injury sustained in a car accident. Of course, he denied being involved, and he wouldn't give any further information on where his godson was.

She shrugged. "I guess it's better to be safe than sorry."

Right. Because I never wanted to experience the fear of losing her again.

We chatted about her follow-up appointment for the concussion the following week, and my first shift back later that same week. Then the usual random type of stuff we always talked about. And by the time she finished her food, it was obvious she was getting tired.

"I can clean up if you want to go in and get ready for bed."

Her eyelids fluttered open, and she nodded. "I'm suddenly exhausted."

"Concussions will do that." I stood and helped her to her feet, taking a few steps with her.

She paused and looked up at me. "I'm good."

I let out a deep breath. She chose to stay with me over her parents because she believed I wouldn't hover. So, as much as it pained me, I nodded and watched her maneuver down the hall toward the guest room.

I carried our plates into the kitchen and began cleaning up. It wasn't long before I heard her calling my name, and I left everything right where it was to venture down the hall to her. Standing in front of her closed door, I knocked. "You need something?"

"Yes. Can you help me, please?"

I opened the door and found Lyla sitting on her bed, face flushed red. She had the sling off, lying next to her on the mattress, along with a T-shirt. I tried not to stare at her legs that were exposed in the short sleep shorts she wore.

"What's wrong?"

"They made it seem so much easier in the hospital."

"What?"

"Getting my shirt off." She huffed. "I don't know if it's because this shirt is too snug or my boobs are just too big. But I can't for the life of me pull it over my head."

I swallowed. *Fuck me.* Was she asking me to help her take her shirt off? Because, honestly, in all the ways I'd imagined taking her shirt off, this wasn't one of them. I just had to hope my dick would respect the situation and behave accordingly.

Coming to stand in front of her, I helped her pull the collar of the shirt over her head. For someone who was in an accident and spent two days in the hospital, I was surprised to find she still smelled good. Her simple scent of vanilla diffused into the space around us. My gaze skimmed over bare shoulders and down to where she held the shirt against her chest.

I cleared my throat and turned away from her. She didn't need me ogling her. I was supposed to be her friend.

Just her fucking friend.

"You good?" My voice sounded husky even to my own ears.

"Um..." she began. "Yeah, I think so."

Thank God. I took two steps toward the door before I froze when she hissed in pain. "Lyla?"

"I'm okay." Frustration and a lack of confidence laced her words.

"Do you want my help?" I would suffer through whatever I needed to if she said yes.

"I'm just tired." It almost sounded like she choked back a sob. "Do you mind?"

I spun slowly. The clean T-shirt sat in her lap, and she looked fucking gorgeous in just the nude-colored bra. Her tits, round and full, held my attention.

Get it together, I scolded myself, attempting to focus on the task at hand.

I picked up the T-shirt, and gently pushed the right sleeve up her arm and the neckline carefully over her head. She lifted her left arm up and pushed it through the other hole. My fingers skimmed down her sides as I pulled the material down, and I froze when I felt her shiver under my touch.

I glanced up at her, and for a brief moment I was sure desire flashed through her gaze. Stepping back, I cleared my throat.

"Thank you," she whispered.

I nodded and turned back toward the door. "Good night, Lyla."

"Night."

I pulled the door shut behind me and adjusted myself. This was going to be a long couple of weeks if I couldn't tamp down my attraction to her.

And why was that suddenly so hard to do?

Chapter Seven

LYLA

"WANT ME TO BRAID YOUR HAIR?" my mom asked as we left my room.

"Oh. Sure. That'd be nice."

Thankfully, I needed minimal help getting dressed this time, but I did need help wrapping my wet curls in an old T-shirt. That was definitely hard to do one-handed. I was learning there were a lot of things that were difficult to do one-handed. But I wasn't about to towel dry it and risk it getting super frizzy. The fabric of the T-shirt would mitigate that problem. Washing my body in the shower proved easier than I expected, but I needed a little bit of help from my mom with washing my hair. Thinking ahead, she'd stopped and gotten me a shower chair, which made the entire process so much easier.

I sat down in one of Adam's dining chairs and my mom began removing the T-shirt. She was quiet as she separated and began braiding my hair. Finally, she asked, "So, you and Adam, huh?"

Based on the knowing look she'd sent me in the hospital when I said I would stay with Adam, I fully expected this conversation to come up at some point. I shook my head. "We're just friends."

"He cares about you."

"Yeah. I care about him too." I pressed my teeth into my bottom lip before adding, "As a friend."

I wasn't about to tell her how my body shivered from his touch last night. I'd convinced myself it was an involuntary reaction. One that surprised us both. And I was nervous things would be awkward this morning because of it. But Adam acted perfectly normal, making me glad the whole exchange didn't make things weird between us.

She was quiet, and I could sense she had more to say.

"What is it, Mom?"

She sighed. "He stayed next to you in the hospital, refusing to leave the room, when you were out. Mia had to bring him coffee and a muffin because he wouldn't leave until you woke up. We were all worried about you, but you could see the fear and anguish in his eyes."

I would likely do the same if he was the one in the hospital. That didn't mean we wanted more than friendship.

"I think you're reading too much into it."

"Time will tell, I guess." The smile was evident in her tone, and I rolled my eyes.

She looped a hair tie around the end of the braid just as the front door opened. Adam walked in carrying a bunch of grocery bags in each hand, wearing a huge smile. "I got everything to make enchiladas and chicken parm, that oat milk creamer you like, and a bag of Sour Patch kids." He set the bags down inside the kitchen and glanced back over at me. "As well as everything you asked for."

"Thank you." I hadn't specifically asked for the oat milk creamer because he had a big bottle of regular creamer in his fridge that I was fine with using. But it was sweet he thought of it.

My mom snickered and then tried to cover it with a cough. "Well, I'd better go."

I held back the eye roll as I stood and gave her a hug. "Thanks for helping me."

"Of course. Anytime." She turned to Adam. "When she's feeling up to it, why don't the two of you come by for dinner?"

"Mom," I moaned.

"What? Least I can do is make the boy a meal for letting you stay here and taking care of you."

She was ridiculous.

"Sure, sounds good," Adam said with a smirk.

Once the door shut behind my mom, I made my way back into the kitchen and started helping pull groceries from one of the bags. "We don't actually have to go to my parents for dinner."

He took the orange juice from my hand. "No, we should. I don't mind, and they'll enjoy it."

I shouldn't be surprised that he cared what my parents wanted. It was just the way he was. Always caring and looking out for people around him.

"Plus," he added, "you know she'll keep pestering you until we do."

That was accurate. And maybe if they saw me doing better and recovering fine, they would worry less and give me some breathing room.

He tipped his chin to the chair I had just vacated. "Sit down and rest. I got this."

I sighed. Which was what was going to make this whole thing so hard. I was so used to being independent and doing things for myself. It was obvious Adam was going to struggle letting me do that. Maybe once I went back for my follow-up next week, he would be better about it.

Regardless, I felt thankful that he was such a good friend and

willing to not only let me stay with him but help me recover as
well.

Chapter Eight

ADAM

Monday 1:22 p.m.

Zack added Seth to the conversation

Zack: So Adam, have you told Lyla you're in love with her yet?

Seth: Why do you keep adding me back to this thread?

Logan: I gave up trying to leave a long time ago. Zack just adds me back in. It's better if you just accept it and silence the notifications.

Seth: Jesus.

Seth: Adam, how's Lyla?

Me: She's good.

Zack: How come you answered his question and not mine?

Me: Because your question was fucking stupid and I'm done telling you we're just friends.

Jay: We're back to that?

Me: Stop riding my dick, fuckers.

Jay: I bet that's not what you're saying to her.

Me: Shut the fuck up.

Seth: Is she remembering anything about the accident yet?

Me: No.

Me: Which is probably a good thing.

Seth: Definitely.

Zack: So...

Jay: Give it up man. He's still in denial.

Me: You both suck.

Chapter Nine

ADAM

LYLA SHIFTED in the passenger seat, pulling my attention over to her. She'd slept a lot in those first few days staying with me, with yesterday being the first day she didn't need multiple naps. She hadn't had any dizziness in the last two days, and only a mild headache, so I assumed her follow-up would go fine today.

It had been almost a week since the accident, and other than some lingering bruises, the stitched-up wound near her temple, and the sling her arm was still in, you wouldn't even be able to tell she was in an accident. Hopefully after her appointment she could start working on getting back to normal, but I would be lying if I said I didn't enjoy taking care of her.

I glanced in the rearview at the car that had made the same last three turns that I had. Maybe I was being paranoid, but I didn't like it. Was someone following us? There was only one way to find out for sure.

I made a right and the car behind us followed.

"What are you doing?" Lyla looked over at me with her brows pulled together.

"I think someone's following us."

She glanced over her shoulder at the car behind us. I made another right and this time they didn't follow. Okay, so apparently I was just paranoid.

She shrugged and relaxed back in her seat. "Not anymore."

But unease settled in my gut five minutes later as a similar blue car pulled out onto the road behind us. "Is that the same car?" I asked out loud, mostly to myself.

"Now you're just being paranoid." I sensed the eye roll in her tone without even looking at her, and I hoped she was right.

"Can you snap a picture of their license plate?"

She scoffed. "I only have one good arm, and it's my non-dominant one. You want me to turn around in the seat and hold the phone steady to get a good picture?"

"Can you take the wheel then?"

Her eyebrows shot up high on her forehead. "Are you serious?"

I glanced in the rearview just as the car sped up, getting a little too close to the bumper of my car for comfort. Would he try running us off the road like he did the ambulance? No way would I let that happen. I made a sudden right and breathed out a sigh of relief when the car didn't follow.

Lyla glanced over her shoulder. "You really think it was the same car?"

I nodded. "Yeah."

We were both quiet as I drove the rest of the way to the hospital. She kept looking around, seeming uncomfortable. That made two of us.

Maybe she was starting to realize that Kyle was right, and was

THE LINE OF FIRE

coming to terms with what I also believed. Whoever ran them off the road actually meant to do them harm.

LYLA

The whole ride to the hospital felt weird. Adam was sure we were being followed, and by the time we arrived, my gut screamed at me that something wasn't right. Almost like that feeling of being watched...or, well...followed.

Maybe Kyle was right.

But the drive home was uneventful, and I was determined to dwell on the positive note from the afternoon. The doctor had given me the all clear—or mostly—to slowly resume normal activities. But only to the point I could handle. I obviously still couldn't use my shoulder yet, not until physical therapy started. But I could start reading and watching TV again. Even take short walks if I felt up to it.

I leaned back against the railing of Adam's balcony, glancing over at him cooking a few burgers on the electric grill he had out there. His outdoor setup was so much nicer than the one at my apartment.

A cooing sound came from above me, and I glanced up, spotting a pigeon sitting on the edge of the balcony above us. I didn't even have a chance to wonder why it was fluffing up its feathers, and, as usual, my reflexes failed me as I watched something drop toward me and land in my hair.

57

My body finally moved and I jumped away from the edge with a squeal of disgust.

"What's wrong?" Adam stared at me with concern in his eyes.

"I'm pretty sure a freaking pigeon just pooped in my hair."

"Seriously?" He stepped toward me as I bent my head forward so he could look at the offended spot. "Only you could have a bird poop in your hair. I'll grab you a wet paper towel."

He chuckled and I whipped my gaze up. "Eww, no. I need to wash it."

His lips lifted into a smirk. "You know they say it's good luck."

"That's great." I rolled my eyes, stalking toward the door and yanking it open. "Doesn't mean I'm leaving it in my hair all night."

I had already showered for the day, but there was no way I was leaving bird poop in my hair for another second, let alone minutes or hours, and a wet paper towel was not going to cut it for me. I didn't want to risk washing it too close to bedtime, either. Going to sleep on wet curls meant waking up to disaster. And a rewash.

Maybe I could handle a quick wash with my good arm before he was finished with the burgers. It didn't hurt to try.

Picking up an old T-shirt from my room to wrap my curls, I headed into the bathroom, feeling more confident in my abilities than I probably had a right to a week post-concussion. Plus, it was no secret Murphy and I were on a first-name basis, that wonderful law of his creating havoc in my life far too often. Still, I'd washed my hair thousands of times in my lifetime. This was the easy stuff. What was the worst that could happen?

After removing my shirt and bra, I grabbed the handheld sprayer and sat on the edge of the tub. I didn't want to put too much pressure on my shoulder by leaning over the side, so this way seemed like a better choice.

Well, until I sat back up after wetting it down.

Reaching out to grab the shampoo, the room started to spin as I was hit with a wave of dizziness. I felt myself slipping off the

THE LINE OF FIRE

edge, but there wasn't anything I could do to stop the inevitable. Fortunately, I was already sitting down, so I didn't have far to go.

The sprayer slipped from my hand and banged against the wall. At least I had the foresight in the moment to protect my bad shoulder, spinning my body so I landed on my back in the tub.

Putting myself right in the path of the sprayer, which was shooting water directly at me.

I clambered against the side, attempting to sit up. No luck there. I slipped back down like a wet fish.

This was going well.

"Oh my God." The water continued to spray my face, everything was slippery, and I couldn't get a grip on anything, especially with only one hand. "Goddammit."

Why did this crap always happen to me?

Fucking Murphy and his damn law.

A knock sounded on the bathroom door. "Lyla?"

Oh thank God. "Help," I called.

The door swung open, and Adam's eyes widened as he took me in. His gaze traveled down to my chest, and he muttered a choked "Fuck" as he blinked slowly, twice, then covered his eyes with one hand and turned away. His eyes caught mine in the mirror, dipped again, and he uttered another strained "Fuck" as he turned toward the door.

It finally dawned on me that I wasn't wearing a shirt. "Close your eyes!" I screeched as I covered my breasts with my good arm.

He pinched his eyes closed and just stood there, rigid and unmoving. What was he waiting for? Maybe he was so surprised my tits were hanging out he didn't realize the water was spraying me in the face.

"Turn off the water," I hollered when he still didn't move.

"How do you want me to do that with my eyes closed?"

Did he not know the layout of his own bathroom?

"Follow my voice. I'll guide you."

He stepped forward and moved his hand along the sink, knocking my curl cream off the vanity.

"Not the sink. Over here." I huffed and tried to cover the spray of water with my foot, which just ended up diverting water to the sides, making even more of a mess. But at least it wasn't spraying right at me anymore.

Slowly making his way toward me, he felt around for the handle, finally finding it and turning off the water. Still keeping his eyes closed, he fumbled around for a towel on the shelf above the toilet and held it out to me.

"Cover up and I'll help you out of the tub. Then you can explain what the hell happened."

Was it not obvious? Why else would I be half naked, sprawled out in his tub. I sighed and covered my breasts with the towel.

"You good?" he asked.

"Yeah."

He opened his eyes and awkwardly tried to help me up, almost like he didn't know where to put his hands and was trying not to touch me.

I felt tears threatening to spill free as a mix of embarrassment and discouragement welled up. "I just wanted to wash my damn hair. Is that too much to ask?"

He stared down at me and I couldn't decipher the look in his eyes.

"Here." He unfolded the shower chair and put it backwards in the tub. "Let me do it."

I shook my head. No way could I ask him to do that. "It's fine. I can wait."

"Lyla." He narrowed his eyes. "Sit down and let me help you."

I recognized the look he gave me. It was the one that said *don't argue*. I let out a breath and sat down in the chair, holding the towel against my body.

As he washed my hair, I tried not to notice how good his hands felt. Because damn did they feel good. Too good.

I shifted uncomfortably. He was my friend who was just helping me out in a bind. I wasn't allowed to be turned on by his touch. We weren't like that.

A moan slipped involuntarily from my lips and I opened my eyes wide in surprise.

He smirked down at me, but then his gaze drifted lower and his pupils flared out. I swallowed, and for a passing second, I wanted to let go of the towel and find out what he'd do.

But then he forced his gaze back on my hair and I felt stupid for letting myself get swept up into a moment that was just a product of a ridiculous situation.

What the hell was wrong with me?

Chapter Ten

ADAM

I ROLLED over onto my back with a huff of frustration. I'd been lying in bed for over an hour, unable to fall asleep because I couldn't stop thinking about Lyla.

Jesus.

Images of her sprawled out in the tub, tits on full display, flashed through my mind for the millionth time. It wasn't even the image of her half-naked body that was burned into my brain. No, it was her little moan of pleasure as I washed her hair that kept playing on repeat in my head.

And I was dying to make her do it again.

Preferably with my tongue, or my hand. Or better yet, as I plowed into her soft, wet pussy.

My dick twitched, obviously loving that idea. I closed my eyes, letting my hand disappear under the waistband of my shorts. My cock was painfully hard as I gripped it and ran my hand up and down the shaft.

Was I really going to jerk off to thoughts of Lyla?

I scoffed. Although, if I was being honest, it wasn't like it would be the first time.

She was supposed to be just a friend. So why couldn't I stop thinking about her as more?

I knew all the reasons we couldn't—or shouldn't—go there, but it didn't stop me from wanting it. And fuck did I want it. So bad. And I had no idea what to do with that realization.

It was probably a good thing I had to go back to work. Even though I wanted to be here with her, I needed some space before I did or said something I couldn't take back.

I continued to stroke myself as I imagined walking into her room and climbing under the blankets, pulling her into my arms. I'd kiss and touch her until I could hear her sweet little moans again. I moved my hand faster as I thought about how I would slowly slide inside her. How she would beg for me to thrust into her. Harder. Faster.

Dammit dammit dammit. This was so wrong. I shouldn't be thinking about any of this, but I couldn't seem to stop either.

"Fuuuuck," I gritted out as the force of my orgasm tore through me.

And that was it. I was totally fucked. Because I thought relieving some of the tension would help me stop thinking about her, but all it did was welcome more dirty thoughts into my head.

I got up and took a cold shower, hoping that would help. But the problem wasn't just sexual. I wanted to hold her in my arms, kiss her, spend every waking moment with her. I wanted to be more than just her friend. The guys were right—I was in complete denial, and I had no idea what to do.

But what I did know was that I couldn't keep pretending I only wanted to be her friend.

~

I CLEARED the top step of the firehouse and glanced around at the guys in the common area. "I need help getting out of the friend zone."

Shocked expressions slowly morphed into smug smirks.

Zack jumped to his feet wearing a huge smile. "About time. I have so many ideas."

I shook my head. "Not taking advice from the only other single guy here. I want to hear their opinions." I pointed at Jay, Logan, and Seth.

Seth shrugged. "Give her a potted plant, or make her a playlist on your phone."

Nope. Neither of those would work. "She'd kill a plant within days, and she already has complete control of my music when we're together."

I looked over at Jay with a raised brow. He'd been so opinionated about us, maybe he'd have a good idea.

"Just keep showing up, man." Jay stood and patted me on the shoulder. "That's what I did with Sarah."

"She's living with me." I wasn't sure I could show up any more than that.

"Just tell her." Logan chuckled. "I learned with Izzy that communication is the key."

That was probably the worst advice. What did he expect me to say... *Hey, I jerked off thinking about you last night*? I cringed. Yeah, that would go over great.

Zack crossed his arms over his chest and cocked a brow. "Want my help now?"

I sighed. His ideas couldn't be any worse. "Fine. What do you got?"

"What made you change your mind?"

That was a good question. But it wasn't that I changed my mind. If I was being honest, deep down I'd wanted this since the moment she walked into my class over six months ago. I'd worked hard to convince myself I was better for her as a friend and coworker, but ever since the accident—and having her in my space —I couldn't keep ignoring how I truly felt. The things she made me want that I never thought I did... It was a lot.

I gave him the simplest answer I could come up with. "I washed her hair for her and we had a moment."

He pointed a finger in my direction. "Then that's what you need. More of those moments of showing her you guys have chemistry that zings off the walls." He dramatically threw his arms out to the sides. With a shrug he added, "Let her catch up to where you are."

I hummed, thinking over what he said. That might actually work. "So you're saying lean into those moments, help her see the attraction."

He nodded and smiled. "And then once you're pretty sure she's on the same page, let one of those moments lead into more."

I could do that.

I started to feel more confident I could pull this off. Until the nerves overflowed as I thought about the possibility that she might not want more.

"Stop that," Zack scolded. "You won't know until you try. Is she worth trying for?"

I stared at him, confident in my answer. "She's worth everything."

"Fuck yes, she is." He walked over and placed his arm around my neck. "Because you're crazy about her. It just took you a little bit to realize it."

How the hell had they all seen it and I didn't? None of that mattered now. I couldn't change the past six months, and I wouldn't even if I could. Being her friend had been exactly what we'd both needed. But now I wanted to show her we could be so much more.

Chapter Eleven

LYLA

"Don't tell me he barged in and saw your ass laid out in the tub." Mia laughed and placed a folded shirt on top of the pile that sat on the bed.

She had organized a schedule between the girls and my parents to make sure someone was here with me when Adam couldn't be. Maybe just a bit of overkill. I was probably fine to stay by myself at this point. But then again, I did get dizzy and fall into a bathtub. Regardless, it was nice to have her help today with things like doing a load of laundry.

I shifted on the mattress and let out a long sigh. "Yup. Tits and all."

She chuckled. "Did he seem to like what he saw?"

I rolled my eyes. "I keep telling you we're not like that."

"If you say so." The smirk playing on her lips said she didn't believe me. "So did you want me to help you wash your hair then while I'm here?"

I shook my head. "No. He ended up washing it for me."

Her eyes widened. "He did?"

"Yup."

"And how was that?" The smirk was back on her face.

I groaned. I shouldn't have even told her. She was sure to make it seem like more than it was.

"Fine." No way was I about to tell her that it felt so good I moaned in pleasure and probably made things awkward as hell. He did act a bit weird before leaving for work, but I was hopeful we would be back to normal once he got home.

"Just fine?"

"Yup." I shrugged. "Just my wounded pride for being such a klutz and then having him see me half naked."

She studied me for a moment, and thankfully didn't push the subject. Just to be sure, I purposely shifted the conversation to her and the guy she was dating. Like her, he didn't want anything serious. I couldn't understand how she did it—relationships with no future. It blew my mind, although it worked for her, I supposed.

After helping me finish folding and putting away the clothes, we tidied up the apartment a bit before she headed out.

As the door closed behind her, my phone vibrated on the kitchen counter. I picked it up, smiling as a text from Adam popped up in the notifications.

Adam: Want me to pick up a pizza on the way home?

Me: Sure.

Adam: Ham and pineapple?

Me: We can do meat lovers. You don't really like ham and pineapple.

Adam: But you do, and I'm good with it.

Me: Why don't we do what we did last time? Half ham and pepperoni and half ham and pineapple.

Adam: That works. See you soon.

I lay down on the couch, just intending to rest my eyes, but must have dozed off because the next thing I registered was the sound of the front door shutting. I slowly sat up, looking over at Adam.

"Sorry. Didn't mean to wake you."

My stomach rumbled. "It's okay. Perfect timing actually. Apparently, I'm hungry."

"Good. I've got hot pizza." He smiled and lifted the box in his hands. "Do you want to finish our game of *Magic* we started last night?"

We'd discovered our mutual love of the collectible card game a few weeks into working together. I'd commented on a post in a Facebook group I had recently joined, not realizing he was in the group too. Talk about your small world. We'd been having weekly games ever since.

As fun as it sounded, my head throbbed at the idea of needing to focus, and I brought my hand up to rub my temple. "Not tonight."

He smirked. "Why? Because you know I'm going to win again?"

I narrowed my eyes. He enjoyed winning way too much. "I just have a bit of a headache."

"Oh." He set the pizza on the counter. "Movie, then?"

"Sure." It could make my headache worse, but it was worth a try.

"Why don't I get us drinks and make us plates while you pick a movie to watch tonight?"

I nodded and finally relaxed, feeling like things were totally back to normal between us.

"You sure you want me to pick?" He knew I had a love for romantic comedies, and there was a new one I had been dying to watch.

"Yeah. I know you've been wanting to see that one based off that book you love."

I smiled excitedly—he didn't even sound disgusted by the idea, or like he was just humoring me— and grabbed the remote. Once I had the movie queued up, Adam joined me on the couch with our drinks and plates. I was surprised he didn't make fun of me again for my strange combo of milk and pizza. He usually gave me shit about it every time.

"What, no teasing me about my milk?"

His lips lifted into a smirk. "I think I've just gotten used to it."

Why did that almost make me feel sad? Was he just saying that because he was handling me with kid gloves since I'd been injured? I didn't want anything to change between us. I liked who we were. Our friendship. Our banter. Hopefully the accident didn't cause a permanent barrier between us.

As we ate our food, I stole a glance over at him a few times. He may never admit it—guy code or whatever—but based on how much he smiled and chuckled throughout the film, I was pretty sure he secretly liked these types of movies.

Finished eating, we relaxed back against the cushions. There were only thirty minutes left in the movie, and I was stifling my third yawn. Considering my unintentional short nap before dinner, I was surprised to find myself so tired again. But concussions could make a person tire easily. This was the first long period of screen time I'd had since the accident, which could be adding to it.

I laid my head back and closed my eyes, just letting them rest for a minute...

ADAM

I chuckled at the male character in the movie. He was so oblivious to his feelings for the girl. Was that how dumb I'd been with Lyla? The thought that maybe I'd missed my chance, and that my plan wasn't going to work, sat heavy in my gut.

I glanced over at Lyla. Her eyes were closed, and I couldn't tell if she was asleep or not. But five minutes later, when she shifted and leaned closer to me, I placed my arm around her shoulders, letting her head come to rest in the crook of my arm.

I held her, savoring the moment for as long as I could. The movie ended, and I stayed frozen in place, afraid if I moved, she'd wake up.

She shifted, nuzzling further into my side, and let out a sigh of satisfaction.

With a smile, I laid my head back. I was aware of her every breath, the weight of her head against my body. Breathing her in, every fiber in my being relaxed. Damn, this felt incredible. So right. This was how I wanted to spend every evening with her. I just hoped she felt the same.

I sensed the moment she lifted her head, and I looked down as her eyes lifted to my face. Instead of pulling away like I usually did, I leaned into the moment, holding her gaze. Tracking the movement of her tongue as it licked along her bottom lip, my body came alive with need, and desire stared back at me.

God. I wanted so badly to kiss her. But I had to remember I

was subtly showing her little moments between us. If I moved things too fast, it could ruin it all.

Her breath hitched, and then she was pushing off me, sitting up as her cheeks flushed.

"I'm sorry." She shook her head. "I fell asleep on you."

I smirked, but I wasn't going to point out that I had my arm around her. "I didn't mind." That was the truth without directly telling her I enjoyed it and wanted more of it.

Her brows pulled together slightly as she studied me, and then she glanced over at the TV. "I missed the end of the movie."

I nodded. "Want me to turn it back on? Or did you want to head to bed?"

She looked back at me, searching my face, and then sighed. "I think I'm just going to go to bed."

My smile slipped. I wanted more time with her, but she also needed her rest. "Okay." I stood and began collecting our plates. "I'll clean up, you go ahead."

"I'll help." She grabbed our glasses, and I followed her into the kitchen.

"I got the rest." I tipped my head toward the hallway. "Go get some rest."

"Alright." She turned and glanced back at me over her shoulder. "Good night."

"Night."

I stood in the kitchen, even more confident than I'd been earlier that this plan would work. All I had to do was slowly show her what we could have.

And then hope to God she would be willing to take a chance on us.

Chapter Twelve

LYLA

Wiping sleep from my eyes, I opened the door to my bedroom and stepped out into the hallway just as the bathroom door swung open. Adam appeared, wearing only a towel around his waist, water dripping down his bare chest.

I could feel the heat creeping up my neck and into my face as I stared at his sculpted torso, my eyes tracing the ink that ran up his arm and over his chest. I itched to reach out and let my fingers follow the same path.

"You're up early," he said.

My gaze whipped to the smirk that broke out on his face. I understood what he said, but for some reason I couldn't form words. I shook my head slightly.

Jesus. Pull it together.

But, damn. Couldn't he put on a freaking shirt?

I tried not to let my gaze drift back down, but failed miserably. The towel he wore hung dangerously low on his hips, showcasing the deep V of his lower abs.

"Lyla?"

I could hear the concern and amusement in his voice and forced my gaze back up to his face. "Yeah... I, um, woke up." I cringed at how lame that was. What the hell was going on with me?

He chuckled and took a step forward. His lips still held a playful smirk, but there was something a bit deeper—darker— shining in his eyes. "I see that."

I held my breath as he stepped even closer. And maybe I was hallucinating, but he seemed to lean down toward me, invading my space.

"Excuse me." There was a deep rasp to his voice that caused heat to pool in my belly. "Can I get to my room?"

What? His room? Oh my God. I glanced over my shoulder toward his bedroom. I was blocking the narrow hallway.

"Oh. Sorry. Yes, of course." I shifted sideways and he squeezed past me.

"Thanks, love."

I froze. Did he just call me *love*? He'd never used that term before. That was... weird. This whole exchange had been weird. Maybe I was dreaming or something.

I let out a breath and chalked it up to strange sleepiness invading my brain, then headed to the kitchen.

Shaking my head to clear the very odd encounter from my mind, I opened the refrigerator, grabbing bacon and eggs to make some breakfast. I wasn't sure if Adam ate anything before going into shift. The guys made breakfast at the station, but I usually had something small before heading in just in case a call came in right away. Did he do the same?

As I placed the last of the bacon on a plate and started whisking the eggs together in a bowl, Adam entered the kitchen. I sensed him come up behind me, so close I could feel the heat coming off him. I stiffened as he leaned forward over my shoulder and reached around me, grabbing a piece of bacon from the plate.

He took a bite. "Mmm. So good."

I stared at his lips as he put the rest of the piece in his mouth. I blinked, breaking the connection and pulling my attention away from him. What the heck was going on with me?

Turning back to the eggs, I focused on getting my lady parts under control. It wasn't like I didn't know how gorgeous he was, I just usually didn't pay it any mind. Because we weren't like that.

So why then was I suddenly super aware of his proximity? The way he smelled. How I couldn't erase the image of his insanely toned chest and stomach from my mind. Not that he didn't look just as hot in his uniform polo he wore now, especially with the top button undone and the sleeves tight against his biceps.

I finally relaxed as he moved away to the other side of the small kitchen.

"Want me to make you a cup of coffee?"

I nodded. "Sure. Thanks."

We moved around the kitchen together, and it all felt so domestic. I couldn't put my finger on it, but something felt different between us.

I turned toward the fridge to put the milk away, then spun back, colliding right into him. His hands grasped my waist and mine pressed to his hard chest. His fingers trailed up my sides, sending a shiver coursing through me.

He smoothed his hands up and down my arms and tipped his head behind me. "Sorry, just need to get the creamer from the fridge."

"Okay." Even though my brain told me to move, my feet didn't obey.

"You good?"

I nodded. "Yeah."

Finally, I forced myself to move around him. I added the eggs to the pan and began scrambling them. Probably with a little too much aggression, but I was frustrated at the way my body seemed to be reacting to him. He appeared next to me, leaning back against the counter and holding a mug out to me.

"Thank you." I took it from him, taking a small sip before placing it down on the counter and finishing the eggs. "You want a small plate?"

"Sure." As he got down two plates, his phone rang from his pocket. He pulled it out and his jaw locked as he looked at the screen. He brought the phone to his ear and walked out of the kitchen, answering with a terse, "What's up?"

I strained to hear his part of the conversation. His voice was low, but it held a lot of frustration. I divided the eggs and bacon between the two plates as he reentered the kitchen.

"Sorry." He reached for the plates, tension apparent in his shoulders now that wasn't there a few moments ago. "I'll carry them to the table."

I followed him with my mug in my hands, waiting until he returned with his coffee and took his seat before asking, "Everything okay?"

He studied me, uncertainty swimming in his eyes. "I'm going to hang out here for a bit before going in."

I narrowed my eyes at him. "Why?"

He sighed. "Dylan said it's probably nothing, but patrol just drove by and spotted a car in the parking lot that matches the description of the one that followed us the other day."

I raised a brow. That was hardly suspicious. There were probably lots of blue cars out there. "Okay..." There had to be more he wasn't saying.

His jaw clenched. "Once patrol pulled into the lot, the car sped away."

"Maybe they were late for work."

He huffed. "If Dylan truly believed that, he wouldn't have given me the heads up."

I couldn't argue with that. He was right. If Dylan called

about it, he obviously thought it might be a threat. Because while he was known to be cautious, Dylan wasn't an alarmist.

"But he has a car out front now, right? So you don't need to stay. I'll be fine."

He shook his head. "They have a make and model and a partial plate and he has all available units out looking."

"I'm safe inside the apartment. What is he going to do?"

Adam's brows shot up to his hairline. "Oh, I don't know. He's a fucking arsonist. Maybe set fire to the building?"

I pressed my lips together into a thin line. There was no need to bring up the fact that he could easily do that with Adam here, or could have done it any time in the last week. I went back to eating my food until he let out a long sigh and I looked back up at him.

"Truth is..." He sighed and scrubbed a hand down his face. "I wouldn't be focused at the station if I was worried about what was going on here. So I'm just going to hang out until Dylan gives me an update."

That I could understand. Being distracted could cost him his life, or someone else's. I sent him a slight smile and nodded. "Okay."

Honestly, I'd never seen him so intense or so on edge before. He was always the levelheaded one, calm under pressure. But as I stole little glances over at him, he seemed anything but those things. I didn't know what to make of it, and it began to make me just as uneasy.

Maybe I could help take his—and now my—mind off the danger he thought was lurking outside.

"Want to continue our game from the other night?" I waved to the cards still sitting on the table.

"Sure." His lips lifted slightly into a smirk. "If you're ready to lose again."

I rolled my eyes. "Just remember, the last time you got cocky, I ended up winning."

"Only because you played that spell that destroyed all my creatures."

"I still won."

"Well, I'm confident you're not winning this one."

He nodded to the table and I picked up my cards. "I guess we'll see, now, won't we?"

Chapter Thirteen

ADAM

LUCKILY, the station wasn't busy, so coming in a little late didn't end up causing any issues. I felt better once Dylan had a car stationed outside. There was no way I could leave Lyla in the apartment by herself knowing the arsonist could be outside watching. I get that me being there wouldn't stop him if he wanted to do something—like set the building on fire—but if I was there, I could at least make sure she got out alive. And like I told her, I would just be preoccupied if I went in, and that was the last thing the guys needed. In our line of work, distraction got you or someone else injured, or worse.

"You've got to be shitting me," Seth said just as I cleared the last step and entered the common area.

Now what?

I followed his glare to Zack, who held up a T-shirt and wore a huge shit-eating grin. I choked back a laugh. The T-shirt design was a red ladder and a black silhouette of a firefighter with the words "save a ladder, climb a firefighter" on it. That was the title accompanying a viral video that had blown up of Seth carrying Violet down a ladder back in August.

"Savannah made them. She's sold a ton already, and she's going to make some for our FD vs PD volleyball game in February." Zach's smile seemed to grow. "Oh, and I told her we'd do a calendar."

"No fucking way," Seth snapped, pushing to his feet and violently shaking his head.

"It's a joint promotion with the local animal shelter." Zack tossed the T-shirt in his hand at Seth. "You saying you don't want to help support all the poor animals that need homes?"

"I'll donate money," Seth clipped.

Chief Thompson entered the common area from the hallway that led to his office. "Need everyone to participate."

Seth's eyes widened as he looked over. "Seriously?"

"We need our portion of the fundraiser for those new face masks you all want." He crossed his arms over his chest. "You want to explain to everyone why we don't have the funds for them?"

Seth huffed but didn't say anything else.

"Jesus." Logan sat up in the recliner, grumbling. "Chief, I'm too old for all that."

"But you're our silver fox. The ladies will go fucking nuts." Zack smirked.

I'm pretty sure Logan growled at him before muttering, "I'm not that old."

Zack shrugged. "Doesn't matter. They all love the slightly-older dad vibe."

I shook my head and headed to the bunk room to put my stuff down as the guys continued to complain about the calendar. I honestly didn't have an issue with it. I had no problem holding a kitten or puppy and posing for some pictures. But then again, there wasn't much I wouldn't do to support the Half Moon Lake FD.

When I stepped back into the room with the guys, they had moved on to discussing details for the volleyball game Zack was pulling together. For the last few years, Zack had managed setting up and organizing all the community outreach programs and events the fire department participated in. He was the most extroverted and organized out of all of us, and when he volunteered to help, the chief was all too happy to take him up on his offer.

"Tickets will go on sale the first weekend in November." Zack looked over at me as I headed across the room toward the coffee pot. "Hey, any update on project kiss the girl?"

I rolled my eyes at the stupid label. The fact that he compared my plan to a scene in a Disney princess movie shouldn't have surprised me, though.

"I think I've got her attention." At least that was my hope after her reaction to me coming out of the bathroom this morning, and then again when I got close to her in the kitchen. Not to mention the questions in her eyes during our moment last night when she woke up with her head on my shoulder.

"Perfect. If she's feeling up to it, do you guys still want to supervise an ambulance at the Touch-a-Truck event next Saturday?"

I nodded. "Sure."

The lights that surrounded the speakers overhead flashed, and we were all moving, knowing the alarms were about to blare and a call was going to come in. Once we were in the truck and headed toward the scene of a car accident, with at least one overturned vehicle, I focused on steady breathing. This was my first crash since being back, and I knew this could bring up memories of the one we responded to involving Lyla. The one where I feared I'd lost her.

"You good?" Logan asked from the driver's seat next to me.

I sent him a clipped nod. "Yep."

"Good. Kyle might need help. I don't think the young buck he's riding with today is gonna last, but hopefully it's just probie jitters."

I nodded. That happened sometimes. Men and women would go through the training, but then not be able to handle the stress and emotional aspect of the job.

As Logan pulled the rig up and I took in the large SUV rolled onto its side, my mind quickly flashed to an image of the ambulance in the same position. I blinked and forced another deep breath into my lungs, pushing all that to the back of my mind so I could focus on what I needed to.

Lyla was fine. Alive. And at that moment, I needed to make sure the same could be said for these people.

Chapter Fourteen

LYLA

"Thank you for doing this." I looked over at Adam as he put the car in park in front of my parents' small farmhouse.

Things between us seemed back to normal, and there had been no more weird moments like the other morning. But there hadn't been many opportunities for a repeat over the last two days, either. He'd left for his shifts before I woke up, and he'd been getting home late as well.

"Of course." His smile had a hint of mischief behind it. "Maybe I can convince your mom to show me some embarrassing but adorable pictures of you from when you were a kid."

Oh God.

My eyes widened almost comically. That was the last thing I wanted to happen. My hair always looked like I stuck my finger in an electrical socket, and my cheeks were always unnaturally rosy, like I'd been running around for hours. Don't even get me started about how my face reminded me of a squirrel carrying nuts.

He laughed as he climbed out of the car, and I rolled my eyes at his ridiculousness.

My mom met us at the door, ushering us inside. "Come on in, dinner's almost done."

"Can I help you with anything?" I asked her as Adam greeted my father.

She shook her head. "No, I don't think so."

I followed her into the kitchen, leaving Adam in the living room with my dad.

After twenty questions about how I'd been feeling, if I was getting enough rest, eating enough, drinking enough, and her concerns about the lingering headaches, I was thankful I'd decided not to stay with them. She barely let me answer a question before she was rambling onto the next one. I loved her and knew she meant well, but sometimes she was exhausting. Finally, I let out a long sigh.

She studied me before her face fell. "I'm sorry. You know me, I worry about you."

I nodded. "I know, Mom."

"Do you want to let the boys know dinner's ready?" she asked as she carried a bowl of corn to the table.

"Yeah."

When I stepped into the living room, they were both fully engrossed in the football game on the TV, yelling about some bad play they both disagreed with. I couldn't help but smile as they followed me back to the kitchen, talking the whole time about how each of the teams were playing.

Dinner started off just fine, but of course I couldn't do anything without a catastrophe following close behind. Almost like it happened in slow motion, my hand swiped Adam's glass of ice water, toppling it over and spilling the contents onto his lap.

"Damn it." I grabbed the napkin from the table and began dabbing at his jeans. "I'm so sorry."

He grasped my hand, pausing my movements just as I realized what I was doing.

"It's okay."

I glanced up at the rasp in his normally smooth voice, and something intense flickered in his gaze. I'd never seen that look before and I didn't know what to make of it. Was he mad?

"See, I told you." My mom snickered.

Reluctantly, I turned my attention over to my parents. My mom smirked at my dad while my dad narrowed his eyes on Adam.

Who knew what she was suddenly gloating about. Probably her theory that Adam and I were more than friends. I rolled my eyes. It wasn't like I spilled water on him on purpose just so I could try to cop a feel at the freaking dinner table.

He shifted uncomfortably in his seat and I cursed my clumsiness. The next five minutes crawled by, the awkwardness lingering until I reached for my own water, nearly knocking it over.

Adam, quick on the draw this time, saved it from spilling. With a smirk on his face, he took one last bite and pushed his plate away. "I bet there were a lot of skinned knees when she was a kid."

My mom nodded dramatically. "Skinned knees, elbows, random injuries, and lots of messes."

I sighed, exasperated at her willingness to overshare. "Way to throw me under the bus, Mom."

Honestly, though, I was thankful his teasing broke the tension.

She chuckled. "But once she started dance classes, it got a lot better."

Adam's brows rose and he turned toward me, placing his arm along the back of my chair. "You danced?"

"Yup." The fact that I didn't constantly topple over while I danced was a constant source of surprise for all of us. And the classes actually helped my coordination, posture, and spatial awareness. "Started in fourth grade and continued all the way through my senior year." I shrugged. "I wasn't the best, but I became pretty good."

"We tried a few sports first. It was...not good." My mom's nose wrinkled like she smelled something bad.

Dad scoffed. "That's an understatement. I swear, I was convinced the ball would purposely seek her out. And it didn't matter what kind. Softball, soccer, lacrosse. She got hit by every single one, multiple times."

Adam cocked a brow at me. "So does that mean you won't be participating in the volleyball game in February?"

"Definitely not." I wasn't stupid enough to even try that. "I would probably end up with another concussion."

"I have a ton of pictures from her dance recitals over the years that I can pull out." My mom smiled proudly.

"He doesn't want to see a bunch of pictures of me as a kid."

"Oh, I totally do." His smile was genuine, but maybe with a hint of mischief. "I need to see proof of this dancing thing."

I swatted his stomach with my good arm. "You're ridiculous."

Part of me was sure he was joking, but twenty minutes later, he sat next to my mom on the sofa as she showed him the dance album she'd created many years ago. I didn't understand why this was important to him. Ammo to tease me with later?

I shook my head and went back into the kitchen to start rinsing the dishes and loading them into the dishwasher.

After a few minutes, Adam entered the kitchen and sidled up next to me. "Here, let me."

"I am perfectly capable of loading a dishwasher." I raised a brow, daring him to challenge me.

"Without spilling water everywhere?"

I gathered a handful of water, throwing it at him and then smirking. "Oops. I guess not."

He took a step forward, that mischief back in his eyes, and reached out, grabbing the sprayer. I quickly moved away from the sink before he could spray me. But he just grinned as he took over putting the dishes in the dishwasher. I huffed and crossed my arms.

Damn him.

He stole a glance over at me. "Did you enjoy dancing?"

"Yeah. I did." I grabbed a dirty glass from the island and brought it over to him.

"You've never mentioned it." He reached out to take the glass from my hands.

Our fingers brushed, and I froze as it sent a zing up my arm. I yanked it back and turned toward the island, attempting to catch my breath.

What the heck was that? I didn't understand why I was suddenly having these moments with him. Maybe the bump on my head was somehow causing these weird things to happen.

Totally possible.

Chapter Fifteen

ADAM

I LEANED back against the ambulance, watching as hordes of kids bounced from one big vehicle to another.

Touch-a-Truck events always felt like controlled chaos. The sirens going off for fun, babies and toddlers crying, parents hovering with phones out ready to snap a picture. We were off duty, but also not really. The ambulance was still ours to watch, and the people were still our responsibility.

Regardless, I liked these days. No calls. No blood. Just kids pretending to be heroes and us pretending not to flinch when someone climbed where they shouldn't. And who knows, maybe one of these events would inspire a future EMT or firefighter or five. Future recruiters and chiefs could thank us.

Lyla had a group of young kids hanging on her every word.

Like them, I was enthralled by her. Parents hung back, chatting with each other, likely happy for the small break. I smiled as she explained for the tenth time that no, we couldn't turn the lights on again.

She finished up with them and they waved excitedly as they ventured on to the next truck. A father and his little boy peeled off from the crowd and headed straight for us. The kid couldn't have been more than six, all smiles and excitement, dragging his dad by the hand.

"Is this a real ambulance?" he asked, eyes wide.

"Sure is." Lyla dropped into a crouch so she was eye level with him. Her voice was familiar. It was the one she used with patients. Steady and warm, like with just her words she could make it all okay. "You want to see the inside?"

The boy nodded so enthusiastically he reminded me of a bobblehead.

The dad laughed, ruffling the child's hair. "He's been talking about this all morning."

I helped the boy up into the back and then reached out a hand to Lyla, doing the same for her. Her injured arm was still secured in the sling and getting in and out of the back proved to be a tad bit difficult for her. She wasn't using the sling around the apartment much lately, but with the crowd and kids who weren't always careful, we felt it was safer to keep her arm secured for the day. I didn't mind having to help her in and out of the ambo. It gave me an excuse to touch her. Plus, after she tried climbing in one-handed earlier in the day and nearly fell back out, I wasn't taking any chances.

She started pointing things out, letting the kid hold the blood pressure cuff like it was treasure. I stayed a step back and only answered questions when asked, watching the way Lyla's long braid swung as she moved. She was enjoying this, and I had to remember to thank Zack. Seeing her back in her element with a smile on her face made me irrationally happy.

"Wow, that's a lot of equipment," the father said, leaning against the doorframe. "You must have nerves of steel."

Lyla shrugged sheepishly. "You get used to it. Plus, teamwork helps," she added, shooting me a smile.

"Still," he said, eyes lingering a beat too long, "I bet not everyone can handle what you do."

Something tightened uncomfortably in my chest. I told myself it was nothing. People flirted with Lyla all the time. She was smart and kind and pretty in a way that snuck up on you. It wasn't new. It shouldn't have bothered me.

But it did.

"Dad, look!" the boy interrupted. Thankfully. "This one's for breathing!"

"That's right." Lyla showed him how it went on. "It's called an oxygen mask."

The father kept his gaze trained on her, pretty much ignoring the fact I was standing a few feet away. "So...do you work a lot of events like this, or are you usually out saving lives?"

I cleared my throat. "We rotate." The words came out a little sharper than I meant them to. "Mostly emergency calls."

He glanced at me for the first time, surprised, like I'd appeared out of thin air, and then nodded. "Right. Of course."

Lyla shot me a quick look, nothing accusatory, just curious, and I immediately regretted speaking. Although I hoped it would change sooner rather than later, I wasn't supposed to be anything more than her partner. Her friend. The guy who handed her gloves and shared bad coffee at three in the morning. Not some jealous boyfriend hovering at her shoulder. And it sure as hell wasn't the way I wanted her to realize my feelings for her either.

"Well," the father said, turning back to her, "if you ever need a break from all that intensity, I know a great coffee place nearby."

There it was. Smooth. Confident. The kind of line that probably worked more often than not. The kind of line I would use. Hell, I'd used similar ones plenty of times. But something about it being used on Lyla made me see red, and if I didn't walk away soon, I might do something I'd regret.

Lyla laughed politely. "That's nice of you."

Not yes. Not no. Just Lyla being Lyla.

I focused on the kid, asking him if he wanted to sit in the captain's chair up front. He scrambled past me, thrilled, and I followed, grateful for something to do with my hands because throttling the kid's father wasn't a valid alternative. That would be difficult to explain to the chief. And probably involve a lot of paperwork.

From the cab, I could still hear them talking, Lyla's laugh drifting in through the open doors. I told the boy about the radio, let him press a button that didn't do anything important, nodded along to his endless questions. All the while, my mind replayed the way the father had looked at Lyla. The way it made me feel. The way I itched to walk back there and tell him to move along.

When they finally stepped away, the boy waving like we were celebrities, Lyla closed the doors and leaned back against the bumper. "Nice family."

"Yeah." I forced my voice to stay neutral. "Kid was really into it."

She jabbed me playfully in the ribs with her elbow. "What's your deal? You seem... tense."

"Nah." I shook my head, willing my shoulders to relax. "I'm fine."

She studied me for a second longer, then smiled and turned to the next group of kids approaching.

I let out a long breath, words I was dying to say still lingering on my tongue. For the hundredth time in the last week, I reminded myself of the plan. I was still just her friend. Her partner. And even though I wanted more, that had to be enough for now.

Chapter Sixteen

ADAM

Monday 6:45 p.m.

Zack: Going out after shift. You and Lyla want to come?

Me: Not this time. She's tired and wants to finish the Magic game we started yesterday.

Jay: *GIF from Revenge of the Nerds*

Zack: Yesterday? You haven't let her win yet?

Me: Why would I let her win?

Zack: *eye roll emoji*

Zack: Because she'll be happy. Bruh, I'm the single guy and even I know that.

Jay: Yeah, that's dating 101, man.

Jay: Don't you know that?

Me: No. I can't say I have ever done that.

Jay: Explains why you're still single.

Logan: Am I the only one not surprised by this? Of course he wouldn't let someone win. He's the most competitive person I know.

Zack: He also gets super pissed when he loses.

Me: Not true.

Zack: So let her win then. She'll be happy and smile and you'll be closer to your goal.

Logan: Bet he won't do it.

Me: Watch me.

Jay: You sure you can?

Me: Shut it.

Zack: Update us when it's done.

7:15 p.m.

Me: There, it's done.

Zack: Good job.

Jay: We might need proof.

Logan: Yeah, I don't believe it.

> Me: *picture of Lyla with a huge smile on her face*

> Me: It killed me to let her win, but her smile made it worth it.

Zack: See? Told you.

Logan: Well I'll be damned.

Zack: You and Jay owe me $20.

> Me: Seriously? You guys bet against me?

Jay: Didn't think you'd go through with it.

> Me: Thanks for the vote of confidence.

Jay: Not confident enough to win me money.

Chapter Seventeen

ADAM

I PULLED the casserole dish from the oven and placed it on top of the stove. Mexican and Italian were Lyla's favorites, and when I told her I could make my mom's lasagna tonight for dinner, her eyes lit up. I couldn't wait to see the look on her face when she took the first bite.

My phone vibrated on the kitchen counter, and I glanced down, thankful to see my mom was calling. Talking to her would take my mind off Lyla in the shower.

Hopefully.

I picked up the phone and swiped the answer button. "Hey, Mom."

"Hi."

"Everything okay?"

"Yeah. Just wanted to see if you were still coming by tomorrow to look at my kitchen sink."

I flinched, having forgotten all about it until she had mentioned it. Which wasn't typically like me, but the gorgeous redhead living in my apartment and taking up permanent residence in my head was one hell of a distraction. "Yep. Probably after lunchtime. Lyla has physical therapy in the morning."

"How's she doing?"

I turned off the oven and leaned back against the counter. "Good. She'll do two weeks of PT and then she should be able to get back to work."

"That's great. Feel free to bring her with you tomorrow. I always love talking with her."

What was she rambling about? When did she talk with Lyla? As far as I knew, they'd only met once when Lyla and I were on shift and picked up lunch at The Dock. My mom happened to be there with a group of her friends.

"What do you mean? When do you talk to her?"

"Oh." She chuckled. "Anytime we run into each other, she always stops and chats with me. She's so sweet."

I smiled. That sounded like Lyla. She was good with people. Would get patients talking and calm better than I could sometimes. And anytime we went anywhere in this small town, she would stop and talk to anyone and everyone. I saw myself the same way, and I liked that we shared that trait.

It worked especially well with our crew. Logan and Seth were quiet and standoffish. Zack was great at making people laugh. Jay was better with kids than adults sometimes. And Lyla and I could easily get people talking about anything and everything.

"Okay. I'll ask her if she wants to come with me."

I looked up as Lyla appeared, locking eyes with her. Her hair was wrapped in a T-shirt and her face was free of makeup. The strong smell of vanilla overwhelmed my senses, and I tried and failed to stop my gaze from trailing down her body. The snug tank top she wore hugged her tits perfectly, and her leggings fit her like a second skin.

"Alright. Sounds good."

My mom's voice pulled me from my thoughts, and I blinked, glancing back up to Lyla's face. Her brows were pulled slightly together as she studied me. As I kept my eyes focused on hers, the tension between us amped up. I was only slightly aware of saying bye and hanging up with my mom, as I was locked in the moment with Lyla.

Her lips parted in a perfect O, and I could only hope that she was seeing the desire in my eyes.

The need to finally make her mine consumed me, but I had to stick to the plan. She needed to realize what lay between us on her own, and decide giving us a shot at more than friends was what she wanted too.

LYLA

A shiver raced through me from the desire in Adam's eyes. I shifted uncomfortably on my feet and looked away. I was being ridiculous. Reading into things. I had to be.

But these moments were getting more frequent, and I couldn't figure out what was going on.

Had something changed between us? Did I want it to?

I refused to look at him again, but the silence was driving me nuts.

"Who was that?" I finally asked.

He shut the refrigerator door and turned back toward me with a container of grated Parmesan in his hand. "My mom."

"Oh." After another moment of hesitation, I stole a glance up at his face.

He smiled—something sweeter than his usual smile. Or maybe I was just overanalyzing every little thing now.

"She said you should come with me tomorrow when I go over there to fix her sink."

"That'll be nice. I love chatting with your mom." Although the break from the looks I couldn't decipher and the weird moments between us didn't sound horrible either.

"Funny, she said the same thing about you."

I shrugged. "She's a lot like you."

"Yeah?" he prompted.

"You know, easy to talk to, funny, kind..."

He smiled at me again and my stomach fluttered. I shifted on my feet, feeling nervous. Like I'd said too much, or went too far. I'd never questioned things between us, but suddenly I felt so unsure about everything. I couldn't put my finger on what had changed, and frankly, I didn't want anything to change.

At least I didn't think I did.

But I also couldn't ignore the weird moments between us in the last two weeks. Or the way my body responded to those moments.

Needing to put some distance between us, I turned and walked the few feet to the table that sat outside the entrance to the kitchen. I surveyed the *Magic* game still set up on the table, trying to understand the move he'd made earlier. Pretty much a hasty attack. He'd said he wasn't paying attention and missed my creature that had an indestructible effect. So now he was down his strongest player, leaving me with a large opening.

None of it made sense. Maybe once in a while he'd make a mistake like that. But not twice in the same week.

"Planning your attack?" He set my plate down on the table and went around to the other side, setting his down.

Maybe he was getting bored with it and that was why he was making sloppy moves. "We don't have to play anymore if you don't want to."

His eyes widened. "What? Of course, I still want to play."

"Okay…" I shrugged.

His forehead creased. "What makes you think I don't?"

I shrugged. "You don't typically make careless moves."

A smirk lifted the corner of his lips. "How do you know I didn't do it on purpose?"

I looked at the board, trying to figure out how the move he made could possibly benefit him. Maybe he had a spell that would allow him to return a creature from his graveyard and give it a special effect.

"Hmm." I sighed. Only one way to find out.

I played the next few rounds very cautiously, but once I felt confident enough, I attacked with my best creature.

"Sorry." He chuckled darkly as he played a card that killed my attacker.

"Ugh." I huffed. "I knew you were holding onto something."

He shrugged. "I always have a plan."

I rolled my eyes, and we continued to play. Finally, almost an hour later, I made one last attack, winning the game.

"That's the second time this week I've won." I couldn't stop my lips from forming a huge smile. It wasn't that I never won. But he had more patience with the long-game strategy than I did and won more often because of that. I liked the action of attacking and playing spells, whereas he worked the entire game to build up his creatures, all the time holding onto one or two spells and then wiping me out in one fell swoop. I knew this, and still I played the way I liked. I enjoyed the action of the plays during the game, and I didn't always need to win.

"I have to up my game."

I chuckled. "Or just stop making insane plays that might not work out."

"Sometimes you gotta take risks in order to win." He sat back, staring at me intently. "Bigger the risk, bigger the reward."

I tilted my head, assessing him. The way he said it made it seem like there was a hidden meaning to his words. Was he saying I needed to take more risks in more than just a game of *Magic*? And what would prompt him to say that? Or was I just reading too much into his tone? Probably the latter.

When I yawned again for the third time in twenty minutes, he stood and tipped his head toward the hallway. "It's late. You're tired. Why don't you go ahead to bed."

I rose from my seat and searched his face. For what, I didn't know. Just a weird feeling that something was left unsaid.

But fatigue had started to settle heavy over my body, and I knew I needed sleep. Tomorrow morning was my first physical therapy appointment, and if I wanted to get back to work in two weeks, then my shoulder needed to be at one hundred percent.

Reluctantly, I nodded. "Good night."

"Night."

After shutting the door to the guest room behind me, I leaned back against it, replaying the whole night in my head. Half scared that something between us had changed, and half intrigued about what it all meant.

Chapter Eighteen

ADAM

REPLACING a faucet shouldn't take very long. But clearly, when you're distracted, it takes a hell of a lot longer than it should. My focus kept being pulled back to the living room where Lyla sat and talked with my mom. The way the two of them smiled and laughed, like they'd always known each other—it made me happy. Gave me hope.

And it made me want to fall to my knees in front of Lyla and tell her how I really felt.

"Don't you agree, Adam?" my mom asked.

I looked up and over the breakfast counter into the living room. "Agree?"

"Yes." She nodded. "How gorgeous this color blue is on Lyla?"

I bit the inside of my cheek to stop myself from saying she was gorgeous in any color. In front of my mom, before I could truly call Lyla mine, was not the time for such a declaration, so I nodded. "It's very pretty."

My mom raised a brow at me before turning her attention back to Lyla. I blew out a breath and got back to my task.

After finishing up with the sink, we said our goodbyes. My mom wrapped Lyla in one of her mama bear hugs, like she was already part of the family. The whole experience made me want a future with Lyla even more than before. It was like I could picture it so perfectly. And the entire drive back to the apartment I itched to tell her how I really felt. That I wanted more than just friendship with her.

When my phone chimed from the center console, I glanced at it and let out a sigh. One that had a hint of annoyance to it.

"What's wrong?" she asked, and I didn't miss the concern in her eyes.

"Chief wants to know if I can come in early for my night shift tonight. They're dealing with a large fire and someone from second shift just got sent to the hospital for burns."

"And you don't want to?"

It wasn't that. Well, not exactly. It wasn't that I didn't want to work. It was that it would be the first night shift since Lyla began staying with me. I was already apprehensive of leaving her alone all night. Adding four more hours to it wasn't sitting right in my gut.

But I couldn't tell her all that. I wasn't sure how she would feel about my need to be with her—to protect her. The last thing I wanted to do was make her feel like I was smothering her. So I shook my head and held back the whole truth.

"Just wanted a few hours to chill at home before I have to go in." I typed out the quick affirmative response to the chief before glancing back over at Lyla. It wasn't like me to say no to picking up extra hours, and I knew Lyla would be suspicious if I did. "I'll need to give Dylan a heads up I'm going in early."

Her shoulders lifted in a slight shrug. "Okay."

I sent one more text—to Dylan this time—and then we made our way inside. Grabbing my duffle, I stood in front of Lyla, who stifled a yawn. Between physical therapy and then being at my mom's, she was probably exhausted. I wrestled into submission my urge to reach out and pull her into me. Wrap my arms around her and breathe her in.

Instead, I resigned to squeeze her shoulder. "You okay?"

"Just tired. I'm going to go lay down."

I nodded. "Good idea."

"Be safe tonight." Her bottom lip disappeared as she pulled it into her mouth with her teeth. Her nervous habit had an effect on me that it shouldn't, and I cursed both her habit and my reaction to it for the millionth time.

"Aren't I always?" Reluctantly, I dropped my hand to my side. "Lock the door behind me."

She followed me to the door and I waited until I heard the click of the lock before heading toward my car. As I started the engine, I took another minute to glance around. Likely it was just my uneasiness at leaving Lyla for the night, but I was struggling to shake the feeling of dread that suddenly washed over me.

IT HAD TAKEN MORE than two hours to get the fire at the large clothing warehouse completely extinguished and the overhaul process complete. With so much cardboard and fabric, it fed the fire faster than our efforts could tamp it down. Since arriving back at the station, we'd begun the process of washing our turnout gear and equipment to decontaminate it.

"Hell of a night," Daniel, one of our young volunteers, said.

I paused my task of wiping down my helmet and glanced over at him. He was covering a vacation for one of the second shift guys. Barely twenty-one, but a good kid with a lot of potential for a great firefighter. Stayed calm, followed orders, and had all the right instincts.

Jesus. Shitty way to kick off the week though. He was the same age I was when I got hired as full-time, and I had a couple of years of volunteering under my belt by then. I thought back on my first intense fire, similar to the one we just finished with, but with heavy machinery and chemicals that made it even more dangerous. I was impressed he handled the large fire tonight so well.

"Yeah," I said. "Hopefully it's quiet for the rest of shift."

My phone vibrated in my pocket, and I pulled it out. Fear raced down my spine as Dylan's name flashed across the screen.

"What's wrong?" I barked out, bringing the phone to my ear.

"Likely nothing…but patrol thought they spotted someone lurking near the tree line when they drove by. I'm going to post Ethan out front to keep an eye on the building tonight."

My muscles tighten with tension. "Did you update Lyla already?"

I was surprised she hadn't texted yet if he did.

"Yes. She's fine. I told her just keep the door locked and don't open it for anyone but Ethan, me, or you."

I tried to relax my shoulders, but nothing about this felt right. Something was screaming at me that danger was lurking outside my apartment.

After hanging up with Dylan, I called Lyla. Hearing her voice instantly made me feel a little bit calmer.

"You ok?" I asked, barely letting her get a whole word out. But I had to hear her tell me she was okay. Then maybe the storm raging inside me would quiet down.

"Yeah." Her voice cracked.

"Lyla?" I flinched at the sharpness in my tone. But she was holding something back and I needed her to tell me the truth.

"I'm scared." She rushed the words out, barely taking a breath before adding, "Dylan said it was probably nothing, but I don't know…I just have this bad feeling I can't shake."

Fuck. That made two of us.

And if we were both feeling the same way, maybe we needed to listen.

"I'm coming home."

"No, you don't need to do that. I'll be fine. Don't worry."

Well, it was too late for that, because there was no way I could stop worrying.

Chapter Nineteen

LYLA

I PACED THE APARTMENT AGAIN, glancing over at the dark curtains that were pulled together in front of the sliding glass door that led to the balcony.

Being one flight up should have made me feel safer.

It didn't.

Probably because when I looked out the door earlier, my gaze shifting to the tree line, I got the distinct feeling that someone was watching me.

Maybe this whole situation was just adding fuel to my overactive imagination.

Adam said he was going to try to come home. Part of me wanted him to. But the other, more rational part of me knew he was needed at the station.

The distinctive sound of a key being turned in a lock caused me to whip my gaze toward the front door. I held my breath until the door swung open and Adam appeared.

He shut the door, and my feet were moving before I could even think about it. His arms opened with an obvious invitation, and I didn't hesitate to take him up on it. I melted against him as he pulled me against his chest, finally feeling safe for the first time in the last hour.

The tension completely left my body as his hand rubbed up and down my back. The touch was simply soothing at first, but quickly morphed into more as my skin heated. Without permission, my breath hitched, and when a groan rumbled from his chest, I pulled back to look up at him.

The heat of his gaze burned into me as it skated across my lips. Was he going to kiss me? Did I want him to kiss me? A mix of excitement and uncertainty rolled through my body at the idea.

He searched my face, slowly leaning down toward me, but paused a breath away. For a moment, disappointment bubbled up. Until he closed the distance and slanted his mouth over mine.

His lips were gentle but demanding as he devoured my mouth. I fisted the back of his shirt, anchoring myself to him, and he tightened his arms around me. Tangling his fingers in my curls, he tilted my head and then parted my lips with his tongue, deepening the kiss. I struggled to catch my breath, so entirely consumed with his kiss.

Jesus. I had imagined this. But nothing I had ever conjured in my waking or dreaming mind compared to this moment.

He mumbled my name in a tone I had never heard from him before. It was needy. Desperate. And I liked it. A lot.

So many thoughts swirled through my head, but before I could grab onto any of them, the ringing of a phone startled me, and worry about the current situation outside shot to the surface.

I wasn't sure if Adam sensed it or not, but he broke the kiss and stepped back, fishing his phone from his pocket and bringing it to his ear.

He stared at me as he answered, still trying to catch his breath, and tracked my movements as I brought my fingers to my lips.

What just happened? And what did it mean?

I wasn't interested in a friends with benefits thing, and I couldn't imagine he would be either. But did that mean he wanted something serious? Was that what I wanted?

If we went there and it didn't work out, it could be the end of our friendship. Not to mention it could be disastrous to our working relationship.

I shifted uncomfortably on my feet as my thoughts continued to swirl, attempting to ignore the feeling of Adam's gaze burning into me.

ADAM

Fuck. I could see the uncertainty in her eyes. Did I just screw everything up? But she wouldn't have kissed me back if she didn't feel the same way I did. And she sure as hell definitely kissed me back.

I was too distracted, only half paying attention to what Dylan was saying on the other end of the line.

"You there?" he asked.

"Yeah." I sighed, wishing I had Lyla back in my arms instead of Dylan in my ear. "Just walked in the apartment."

"That's what I was just saying." He huffed. "Ethan called me saying you were back. I thought you were working the night shift?"

"I was." I shook my head, technically *still* was. "I mean, I am."

"Okaaay…"

Maybe I was hyper-focused on Lyla at the moment, but I was struggling to comprehend what he needed from me.

"So why are you home now?" He spoke like he was gritting his teeth and trying not to snap.

That was fine, because I was right there with him. And I had no plan to sugarcoat my response. He needed to know my intentions.

"No way was I leaving Lyla here by herself with some lunatic out there watching the apartment."

Her eyes cut to me, studying my face.

"We don't know that—" he began.

"Doesn't matter." I cut him off, and hoped I could convey the meaning behind my next words as I stared at Lyla. "What if it were Hattie?"

Her brows pulled together.

Dylan let out an exasperated sigh. "That's not really the same."

"It's exactly the same. In every way imaginable. No way was I leaving Lyla, just like no way you would leave Hattie."

Her mouth dropped open, and at least now I could see more clarity in her eyes.

"Noted. Just no trying to play hero, got me? Let us handle it."

My grip tightened on the phone. If it came down to protecting her, I'd die trying, so I wasn't sure I could make any promises.

"Call me back if you have an update. I'll be here."

Hopefully, with Lyla wrapped in my arms.

I hung up and shoved my phone back in my pocket. There

was so much I wanted to say, but I didn't have the first clue where to start. After the way she responded to my kiss, there was no denying she wanted more. But she needed to understand what I wanted. Because it wasn't just her gorgeous body for some short-term hookup.

"Lyla..." I began.

Her teeth sunk into her bottom lip so hard I was surprised she didn't draw blood. I stepped forward, bringing my thumb and forefinger up to grip her chin and gently prying her lip free.

"I want so badly to finish what we started." I slid my hand around to cup the side of her face. "But I need you to know that once I have you in my bed, you'll be mine. In every sense of the word. Not just my friend, but the only woman I've ever imagined a future with."

Her eyes widened slightly. Was she not expecting that? Or had I gone too far with my truth? There was so much at risk, I understood that, but I was ready to lay it all out for her and prayed she felt the same.

"I—" She visibly swallowed and pulled her gaze away.

I wasn't willing to accept that she didn't feel the same. Deep down, I knew she did. But I also knew she was busy assessing the possible fallout in her head.

"Love," I whispered, rubbing my thumb back and forth along her cheek. Once she met my eyes again I continued, "You're so damn important to me. And if you tell me you don't feel the same, I'll go back to being just your friend. Because I can't imagine not having you in my life." Honestly though, and maybe I was overly confident, I didn't believe she could utter those words. And if I had to, I would continue to show her how amazing we could be together until she realized it too.

"I don't understand..." She slowly stepped back out of my hold, shaking her head.

What didn't she understand? I thought I was laying it out pretty clearly for her. I couldn't think of any other way to be clearer.

But before I could say anything, she asked, "Have you felt this way the whole time?"

My stomach bottomed out at the hint of suspicion in her voice. I roughed a hand down my face. I wouldn't lie to her.

"Yes." I paused when she gasped, but then rushed the rest of the words I needed to say out. "But I convinced myself I was better for you as a friend. I've never been interested in a future with anyone. Never saw myself as that type of guy." I shrugged.

"And now?" She cocked a brow.

"Now all I can see is you." I silently cheered when her lips lifted into a smile. "After—" Emotion rose to the surface as the words got stuck in my throat. "After the accident...I started to realize it's you next to me that I see in my future."

"We probably wouldn't be able to ride together."

I bit back a chuckle at the way she pouted at that idea. Frankly, I hated that too. Riding together as partners was something we both enjoyed.

"Probably not." I stepped forward and ran my hands up her arms. "But you never know. We're a small station and short on staff. Chief might not have a choice sometimes but to pair us together. But you're right, we wouldn't be able to in the same capacity we have been."

An air of hesitancy still lingered around her. Maybe I admitted too much. Regardless, I needed her to be sure. Because I was damn sure.

I searched for the right words, but a heartbeat later, loud shrieking alarms sounded from the hallway. My body tensed. The last thing I wanted to do was take her outside, especially if this was the arsonist trying to lure us out.

I walked to the door, placing my hand on it to feel for heat. After feeling nothing, I checked the peephole and then opened it enough to see down the hall. The slight smell of smoke hung in the air. Almost immediately, the alarms in my apartment went off too and the emergency lights kicked on.

Now I had no choice. There was obviously a fire, and we couldn't stay in there.

I grabbed Lyla by the hand and led her into the hallway. Tenants from the other units on the floor stepped out into the hallway to investigate, some already heading straight for the stairs.

"Need to evacuate," I yelled loudly.

Lyla and I joined the crowd descending the stairs. Smoke billowed out from the end of the first floor where the laundry room sat.

I pulled Lyla into my side, placing my arm tightly around her shoulders as we stepped outside. The patrol car was still in the same position it was when I'd arrived home.

What the hell was going on? If this was the arsonist, was he suddenly bold enough to try something with Ethan still sitting out here watching the building? This would be a huge escalation for him. Or was he just sending a message? A message that he could still get to her.

Was I letting my suspicion get ahead of me? Lead me to an overreaction or rash decisions. Maybe it was just a simple dryer fire and not the work of the arsonist.

Either way, there was no way we were hanging around out in the open to find out.

Ethan appeared on the sidewalk. "What's going on?"

"A fire on the first floor, maybe the laundry room." I glanced around as I weighed my options. "I'm taking her to the firehouse."

Ethan nodded. "I'll call Dylan and make sure everyone is out." He waited until we were in my car before turning around and running into the building.

"The fire station?" Lyla glanced over at me as I drove the car out of the lot.

"Yeah, he won't try to set that on fire."

She raised a brow. "You sure?"

I sighed. At least I didn't think he would. That would be pretty fucking bold.

"Do you want to leave town?"

She shook her head. "No."

"Cause I have no problem driving us to the airport and putting us on a plane to the other side of the country."

She smoothed her hands down her thighs. "The station is fine."

Our quint truck, the one we used most often here since it was a combination of a pumper and ladder truck, perfect for small towns, flew by us heading toward the fire.

She gasped, and her head turned from the rig back to me, like she'd just realized I was still technically on duty. "Shouldn't you be there to help them with the fire?"

"No." I shook my head. "You're my priority right now. Making sure you're safe and stay that way."

She stared at me and then finally let out a long sigh. So much resignation, but also a bit of gratefulness hung on that sigh. Then she was quiet throughout the rest of the drive.

My thoughts were anything but silent as the things left unfinished between us—the frustration and fear of not knowing where she stood—as well as the threat lurking out there flooded my brain.

LYLA

Being back at the station felt weird. The last time I was there was right before the accident. I pushed away thoughts of that day. So far, I couldn't remember much anyway.

I looked around as we entered the bay. Our main truck was gone, and the building was quiet. The crew was likely at Adam's putting out the fire.

Exhaustion sat heavy in every part of my body. It had been a long, stressful day, and it looked like it was going to be a long night as well.

I followed Adam up the stairs. He looked back at me as I slowed, fighting a yawn with zero success.

"We should probably try to get a bit of sleep before the guys get back," he said, spinning to face me as we stepped into the common area.

I nodded. Sleep sounded like a great idea. "Yeah, I need to lie down for a bit."

Once in the bunk room, he stopped at his bunk. It was already made. I had almost forgotten he was supposed to be on duty tonight. I glanced around. Maybe I could just rest on an unmade bunk. Or one of the chairs in the common area.

He lifted his blanket with a wave. "Climb in."

I raised a brow and looked cautiously around the room. He wanted to share his bed?

"Nothing's going to happen," he added quickly. "I just want to hold you, and I don't want to let you out of my sight."

With a few words, I could've ended whatever we'd started earlier. But was that what I wanted? It appeared my decision was made when no part of me could utter those words.

Climbing in, I scooted over, leaving what I hoped was enough room for Adam. These bunks were definitely not made for two.

Laying down next to me, Adam wrapped his arm around my shoulder and brought me close to him. I breathed him in as I rested my head on his chest. His crisp, clean scent that always reminded me of a day on the water invaded my senses. And with my arm draped over his torso, it was impossible to ignore the muscles that lay beneath.

God, this felt good.

"We can take this slow, Lyla," he whispered. "I wanted you to know how I feel, but I need you to be sure this is what you want before anything happens between us."

I nodded, needing time to digest all of this. The thought of being with him was half exciting and half scary. I let myself inhale all that was him, comforted by his heartbeat and his soothing embrace, as I started to drift peacefully off to sleep.

∾

MY EYELIDS FLUTTERED OPEN AGAIN SOMETIME LATER as noise from the guys filling the common area filtered into our space. I raised up on my elbow and looked down at Adam.

He smiled sleepily at me and reached up, tucking my hair behind my ear. "I could get used to waking up like this."

Would I ever get used to the adoration and desire aimed at me? Based on the way my stomach was flipping from his touch and intense stare, I wasn't sure I ever would. But I totally liked it, and craved so much more of it.

"I guess we should go get an update," he added as his lips formed a tight line.

"Probably." Although I questioned if I wanted to know.

He stood, helping me up, and we headed toward the common area. Once we stepped into the room, the guys all spun to look at us. The silence as everyone stopped talking at once was jarring. They glared at Adam with annoyance, except for Zack who had a smirk on his face.

Jay crossed his arms over his chest. "Next time there's a fire in your apartment building, shoot us a text and let us know if you're going to leave the scene."

"Sorry." Adam flinched. "I told Ethan what my plan was."

Zack smirked. "He updated us...eventually."

"It was a bit chaotic." Logan shrugged. "He had to deal with a drunk idiot who refused to evacuate, and then Dylan showed up."

If Dylan was there, that meant it wasn't an accident. I waited for the news I sensed coming, still not sure if I wanted to know or not.

"So... not a simple dryer fire?" Adam asked.

"Definitely not." Seth shook his head with a frown. "Trash can."

"Maybe someone was smoking and threw the cigarette in there." At this point I was grasping onto whatever I could. Anything that would indicate it was an accident and not malicious intent.

All eyes turned to me with sympathy, and my hope vanished.

"Not likely," Jay finally said. "Dylan and Ethan found evidence of forced entry into the vacant basement apartment."

"Fuck," Adam gritted out.

"Good news is it didn't do any real damage." Zack's cheerful tone stood out among the seriousness of the rest of the room. "You should be able to get back into the apartment tomorrow afternoon."

I swallowed down a gasp. The idea of staying in Adam's apartment by myself caused my heart to hammer in my chest.

As if Adam could sense my dread, he reached out and ran his hand up and down my back. "Don't worry, we'll stay here for now until I can figure something out."

I nodded. Was it too late to take him up on the offer to leave town?

Zack's brows pulled together as he studied us, then the corner of his lips lifted into a smirk. "I'll call my parents. I'm sure they'll let you guys come stay at the lodge. It's gated, plenty of people and security."

I'd almost forgotten that his parents owned a small resort in the mountains only thirty minutes away. Would we be safe there? The apartment building had plenty of people too, and look how that turned out.

"That's not a bad idea." Adam pulled his phone out of his pocket. "I'll call Dylan and see what he thinks." He glanced down at me, his hand still rubbing my back. "I'm going to make a cup of coffee. You want one?"

"Sure, thanks."

Adam walked over to the coffee maker, and I sat in one of the chairs, slowly starting to relax. Maybe the lodge would be safe. If anything, it made me feel better than going back to Adam's place.

Chapter Twenty-One

ADAM

"I HOPE A QUEEN ROOM IS ACCEPTABLE." Zack's dad paused his task of setting up the key cards and looked up at me over the check-in desk.

Speechless, I stared at him, trying to understand what the alternative would be. I'd been here enough growing up to know all the different room layouts. There were three as far as I knew— king suites, queen suites, and double queen rooms.

"I really hoped I could get you two into one of our king suites," he continued, "but they're all booked for the next week." His lips lifted into a smirk. "But I think you'll be happy with the queen suite. It has a jacuzzi tub and fireplace."

"Suite?" I swallowed.

"Yeah. When Zack explained the situation with you and your

girlfriend, he asked if I could get you two into one of the king suites. Unfortunately, I couldn't, but I promised him I'd get you into the queen."

I held back my eye roll. But honestly, I didn't know if I wanted to strangle my best friend or thank him.

I glanced over at where Lyla and Zack's mom sat chatting. Based on Lyla's smile, you would never guess anything was amiss. But I knew she was stressed and exhausted over this whole situation. Hopefully being at the lodge—somewhere detached from the current chaos—would allow her to relax and get some rest.

Returning my attention to the desk, I warred with telling Don that his son had lied, and I would need two queen beds. But deep down, I didn't think it would be a lie for long. And I didn't believe we would really need two beds. After being so close to her in the bunk at the station, even if we took things slow sexually, I still liked the idea of falling asleep with her in my arms. But would she feel the same?

"We're just happy you had a place for us," I assured him with the most grateful smile I could muster.

He gave me a tight-lipped smile, nodded, and handed me the key cards. "Room 205."

I blinked, hesitating before finally making my mind up and taking the cards from him. "I really appreciate you helping us out."

"It's what we do for family."

I smiled. Technically, we weren't family. Not blood relatives, anyway. But my mom had worked there in her teens and through her twenties. It was how she met my father. The company he'd worked for had stayed there for a retreat. After a whirlwind romance, she'd followed him back to his hometown.

When a car accident claimed his life before I hit my first birthday, my mom moved back home, living with my grandparents again and got back her job at the lodge. The Stoers had convinced my mom to bring me to work with her, and their nanny had helped take care of both Zack and me. We became inseparable as toddlers, causing chaos and starting our lifelong friendship.

When I was almost five, my mom started dating Clive—my sister's father. But within the year after Janet was born, they parted ways and my sister only lived with us half the time. My mom liked to say she and Clive were better as friends. I think she still believes my father was her one and only love.

At the start of my third-grade year, she left the lodge and became a secretary at my elementary school, where she still worked. But my friendship with Zach was solid at that point, our families forever joined by a mutual need to care for each other, no matter the circumstances.

After finishing up with Zack's dad, I turned and headed toward Lyla. She looked up at me with a smile that didn't quite reach her eyes. One that held a hint of uncertainty.

"Ready?" I asked her.

Zack's mom stood, offering me a hug. "Just let us know if you need anything."

"I will. Thank you, guys. Again."

"Anytime."

Once in the elevator, I turned toward Lyla with my best don't freak out smile. "So…"

She sighed. "I have a feeling I don't want to know whatever you're about to tell me."

I chuckled. "The room only has one queen bed."

Her brows rose high on her head. "That was awfully presumptuous of them."

I shifted my weight and fought a smirk. Should I throw Zack under the bus?

Absofreakinglutely.

"Not when their son told them you were my girlfriend."

Her hands landed on her hips and her eyes narrowed. "And why would Zack tell them that?"

"Because he's a jackass who likes to meddle."

"I'll make sure to thank him next time I see him."

I cringed. Hopefully that would be sincere by the time she saw Zack again.

The doors to the second floor opened, and she followed me down the short hallway. I swiped the key card and held the door open, letting her step into the large open room.

I almost knocked her over as I walked in behind her. She barely made it in the door before she stopped suddenly. Her breath caught as her eyes scanned the room. I forgot how romantic the suites were, with the cozy sitting area in front of the fireplace and the large jacuzzi tub that sat in front of the floor-to-ceiling windows with a gorgeous view of the mountainside.

"This is..." she whispered, turning to look at me. "Beautiful."

I stared at her, fighting the urge to tell her I thought she was beautiful.

Her cheeks turned pink as I continued to hold her gaze. I didn't want to push her or rush her to embrace us, but I also didn't feel the need to hold back my feelings anymore.

I dropped our bags and reached out, tucking a curl that glinted red in the lights above her behind her ear. Her eyes drifted shut, and a shiver tore through her as I trailed my fingers down her neck.

"You're beautiful," I murmured, leaning forward and pressing my lips to her forehead.

The tension she'd been holding onto all day seemed to melt as her body relaxed under my touch. I wrapped my arms around her shoulders and pulled her into me, tucking her head under my chin.

Happiness enveloped me as I held her, breathing in her intoxicating vanilla scent. She stiffened ever so slightly in my arms, and I smirked. Typically, I would have released her and stepped back by now, knowing holding her was causing a very physical reaction. But I was done hiding the way she affected me.

She squirmed, causing a groan to slip through my lips. I couldn't stop myself from imagining what it would feel like to claim her mouth again. To pick her up, guide her legs around my waist, and press her against the wall.

As I scanned the room, ten more things I'd like to do zipped through my mind. I cleared my throat and released her as I felt her start to pull away.

"Want to go downstairs and grab dinner?" I rushed out, suddenly needing to get out of this room. It was late and neither of us had eaten since breakfast at the station. By the time we got back into my apartment, packed bags and made it up here, it was well past dinner time.

"Sure. And then I need a shower. I feel gross."

She certainly didn't smell gross. In fact, she smelled fucking amazing.

Damn. Now I was imagining her standing under the spray of the shower, completely naked behind what I knew was a see-through glass door, water cascading down the curves of her body.

I swallowed a groan and grabbed her hand. "Okay. Let's go."

Food. Maybe after eating something, I could think more clearly. Or less clearly, depending on how I wanted to look at it.

Chapter Twenty-Two

LYLA

Friday 7:50 p.m.

Me: OMG. We just got to the lodge and there's only ONE bed!

Me: Oh. And a big-ass jacuzzi tub and a fireplace.

Mia: GIF of a woman laughing hysterically.

Nicole: Well, that might make your plan of taking things slow super hard.

Me: It didn't help that he held me and called me beautiful.

Izzy: Aww that's sweet. Maybe he wants to take things really slow too.

Mia: He's a man. Let's be real.

Me: Yeah... so... it was obvious what he was thinking. And I don't think slow was it.

Nicole: Poor guy.

Me: What? Him?

Nicole: Well, yeah. He's been pining for a girl for months, waiting for her to notice him. She finally does, and he's thrown into a super romantic situation with her, but she's still unsure what she wants.

Me: That's not what I said.

Mia: That sounds like a him problem. Not Lyla's. He's had months to tell her how he feels.

Izzy: It sounded to me like he's just recently realized he wanted more.

Mia: Again. That's his problem.

Nicole: Ok, yeah. But I can still feel a little sorry for the guy.

Izzy: Maybe spending time together in a romantic setting will help Lyla realize Adam is what she really wants.

Chapter Twenty-Three

LYLA

JESUS. I set my phone face down on the table with a thud, startling Adam and causing him to whip his gaze from his menu up to my face.

I smiled. "Sorry. The girls just wanted to make sure we got here safe."

He raised a brow, like he wanted to challenge me, because we both knew they could be a lot sometimes, but after a moment he went back to looking at his menu.

My friends were obviously not going to be any help. They were probably still having their own conversation. When I'd updated them this morning with what happened last night with Adam and the arsonist, I never said I didn't know what I wanted. Not sure where they got that from. All I said was I needed time.

There was a lot at stake. The thought of losing Adam in any way was enough to make me sick to my stomach. What if we rushed into something and it didn't work out?

But did I want to know what it felt like to have his lips on mine again? To feel his hands and his mouth roam my body. Or his cock moving in and out of me while I ran my hands over his muscular back and shoulders. Dug my fingers into his ass.

I shifted in my seat as desire throbbed between my legs. Because, yes, I definitely wanted all of that. And more.

"Lyla?"

I glanced up at Adam. He wore a concerned expression, leaning his muscular inked forearms on the table.

"Yeah?" The one word came out breathy. Heat crept up my neck and into my face.

He leaned further across the small table with a smirk. "Have you decided what you want?"

Did he know what I was thinking about? I bit the inside of my lip to stop myself from letting it slip that he was what I wanted. He tipped his chin toward the menu in my hands and my face heated even more at the realization he meant what I wanted to eat.

"Uh, not yet. Sorry." I lowered my gaze and focused on the choices, trying to ignore the feeling of his stare burning into me.

The waiter showing up and taking our order only gave me a quick reprieve. Then I was right back to being aware of his gaze locked on me.

"You okay?" he asked.

"Yep." I cringed at how squeaky my voice sounded. Why was I being so ridiculous?

"Lyla." He reached across the table and grasped my hand. "Relax, love."

God. Why did that one word make me feel all warm and tingly? It didn't help that it rolled off his tongue so easily, like he'd been calling me that for months.

"Just talk to me." His thumb brushed back and forth over my

skin, leaving a tingling sensation in its wake. "Like you always have."

Did he not understand that I couldn't even think straight right now? That the way he kept looking at me, the way he touched me, was turning my brain into mush?

He squeezed my hand, grabbing my attention again. "Are you excited to help with the photo shoot this week?"

I smiled and nodded. Apparently, Zack had assigned Violet and me to help with the dogs and kittens from the shelter. "Totally excited. I'm all about getting to hang out and play with some animals."

He shook his head with a chuckle. "Yeah, I told Zack you'd be up for that."

"I have physical therapy that day, so we're just planning to go right from there to the shoot?"

"That's what I was thinking. Maybe grab a bite to eat between the two."

As we waited for our food, we filled the time talking about the rest of the week. Specifically, his work schedule and my physical therapy schedule. By the time the food came, I was no longer a nervous mess. Things once again felt normal between us, like they always had. But as we walked back to the room after sharing a great meal with comfortable conversation, the worry crept back in.

Would it be weird to share a bed? It wasn't weird last night. But even I could admit the circumstances were different. Nothing was going to happen in the firehouse. Here though, in the privacy of our hotel room, it definitely could.

Did I want something to happen? Maybe the girls were right and I had no clue what the hell I wanted.

Dammit. I was starting to find myself annoying. I could only imagine what Adam thought.

My thoughts continued to spiral even as he unlocked the door and we stepped inside. I needed space, and some time to think.

"I'm going to get in the shower," I blurted, making a beeline for my duffel that sat on a chair.

Rummaging around, I picked out my sleep shorts and tank, and then froze, staring at them. *Shit.* I always dress super cool for sleep. If not, I wake up drenched in sweat. Obviously, I never considered we'd be sharing a bed, but maybe I should have packed something else.

"I'm not going to wash my hair, just my body."

He groaned and I cringed, pinching my eyes shut as I replayed those words in my head.

Just shut up, Lyla. Stop talking.

I spun, clothes in hand, and hurried past him to the bathroom. Once the door was shut, I let out a long breath and leaned back against it.

I took my time in the shower *and* with my thoughts. In the end, I decided it was okay that I needed some time to figure things out. I wanted to be sure because a lot was at stake.

Adam was already under the covers, engaged in his phone, when I stepped back into the room. I shifted on my feet, pulling the shorts back down my thighs as far as I could. He looked up at me, and his pupils flared.

My skin warmed as his gaze ran over my body. There was no way I could deny I liked the heat in his eyes. Making my feet move, I climbed into the bed. Last night, I laid on his chest and snuggled into his side. Could I dare to hope he would do that again? Or was that simply a byproduct of the circumstances?

As usual, like he could read my mind, he put his phone on the end table and reclined back, reaching his arm out. "Can I hold you again?"

I nodded and scooted over, laying my head on his chest.

"Good night, love."

And that warm feeling low in my stomach was back. "Good night."

Chapter Twenty-Four

ADAM

LYLA SHIFTED in my arms as I slowly stirred awake. Waking up with her curled against my body made my chest ache with happiness. I glanced down at her, taking in her long eyelashes laying flush against cheeks that had a dusting of freckles across them. Her dark auburn curls framed her face, and I reached up, brushing them back so I could see even more of her.

She stirred and looked up at me with a sleepy smile. And when her gaze veered down and locked on my lips, the need to kiss her overwhelmed me.

I lowered my head, my intention a simple, chaste kiss. But I should have known better.

Just like the first time, it heated quickly. Her fingers dug into my side as she arched her neck, tilting her head further back and allowing me to deepen the kiss. I tangled my fingers in her hair and explored her mouth with my tongue.

Desire pounded through me. Images of her writhing beneath me raced through my head, and I rolled her onto her back, hovering over her. Our tongues moved together in a hot, sensual dance. My thigh was wedged between her legs, and my cock pulsed, pressing against her hip. As I devoured her mouth, I trailed my hand up her side, cupping her breast, and grazed my thumb over her nipple.

She moaned and arched into me. I could feel the heat through her tiny sleep shorts pressing against my thigh.

Dammit. I promised her we'd take this slow. That I'd give her time.

Reluctantly, I broke the kiss. I moved my hand back down her side and raised up on my elbow to look down at her. "We should probably get up and get dressed."

Her forehead wrinkled in the cutest way. And I felt the same confusion, because every bone in my body wanted to stay in this bed with her.

"We need to be downstairs soon."

Her mouth parted slightly, and clarity shone in her eyes. "Oh, right. Who are we meeting again?"

"Darius. Head of security." Dylan had brought him up to speed yesterday. He'd agreed to brief his team and have them on high alert, keeping an eye out for anything—or anyone—suspicious.

I brushed my fingers along her jaw and down the column of her throat. She shivered, heat gathering in her gaze as I leaned down, just wanting to feel her lips against mine one more time before we had to get up. Her pulse beat hard under my palm as I moved my lips slowly over hers.

I hated to do it, but I tore myself away and pressed a quick kiss to her forehead before rolling over and getting out of bed. My cock was painfully hard, and there was no way I was leaving this room anytime soon.

"I'm going to take a quick shower." Maybe—hopefully—a cold shower would help. I didn't think I had time to do what I really wanted—*needed*—to do.

She nodded. "Okay."

The slight hint of disappointment in her voice made it harder for me to walk away, but before I admitted exactly what I wanted to do with her, I made a hasty retreat to the bathroom.

Thankfully, the cool water did the trick, but within seconds of exiting the bathroom I was right back in the same predicament. The blue sweater Lyla had changed into almost matched the exact color of her eyes. It dipped low, revealing an ample amount of luscious cleavage, each swell of her breast on display.

I licked my lips, and my cock pulsed again, demanding to be acknowledged, freed, and attended to. I adjusted myself with a groan, and when her gaze tracked the movement, a gasp passed through her parted lips as her eyes widened.

Did she still not get it? I closed the space between us, gripping her hips and pulling her against me. She braced her hands on my chest, craning her neck to look up at me, the same look of surprise still on her face.

"For months, I've had to tamp down and hide the way you affect me. But not anymore." With my fingers digging into each of her ass cheeks, I pressed my hardened length tighter into her. "Feel what you do to me?"

She nodded and ran her hands up my chest, making my body come alive with even more need. Lacing her fingers together behind my neck, her surprise slowly morphed into desire, and I internally cheered. I forced myself to not lean in and claim her mouth again, wanting nothing more than for her to initiate. Give me some clue she felt the same.

When she lifted up onto her tiptoes and slanted her mouth over mine, I closed my eyes and that little internal cheerleader did backflips. Matching her pace, slow and gentle, I held back the impulse to lift her in my arms and press her against the wall.

She pulled away, and I wasn't sure if I was relieved or disappointed. I wanted her so bad it hurt, but I also didn't want to push her too far, too fast. And I sure as hell didn't want our first time to be a quickie against the wall.

She sent me a saucy smile, turned, and with a little more sway to her hips, headed out into the hallway. Pausing to adjust myself and will my dick to calm the fuck down, I followed a second later.

The twenty-minute conversation with Darius did very little to lessen my unease about having to leave Lyla and head back to work. Even though his team seemed capable, the conversation was a reminder of just how big the property was and how many people go in and out all day. But I couldn't bail on another shift and leave the crew a man down again.

"Don't worry," Darius said, pulling my attention back to our conversation. "We'll keep your girl safe."

My girl. I loved the sound of that. And taking in Lyla's slight smile out of the corner of my eye, I hoped she liked hearing it even half as much as I did

AFTER ZACK'S mom showed up in the lobby and swept Lyla away to have breakfast with her, I headed to my car. The almost thirty-minute drive would take some getting used to since my apartment was less than ten minutes from the station.

I parked my car in the back lot and got out. A moment later Zack fell into stride next to me.

"How's the room?" he asked, a smirk plastered on his face.

I huffed. "It didn't go like you hoped it would, if that's what you mean." He probably had some half-cocked idea that sharing a bed would lead to sex, but that wasn't my ultimate goal. I needed her to be sure of us first. To be sure of our future.

"Not yet, but it'll help." He chuckled. "And you're welcome, by the way."

"I don't think Lyla wants to thank you, that's for sure."

"Secretly she does, she just doesn't want to admit it yet."

I spun to face him with a scowl. "Maybe, but I promised her we could take things slow. The last thing I want is for her to make a decision out of some forced proximity or obligation and then regret it." I took a deep breath, trying to keep my composure. But I needed him to understand. "Because that will destroy me. I get you were trying to help, but from here on out, I need you to butt out."

His eyes widened and he shook his head. "I'm sorry, man. You didn't tell me you guys talked or anything. I was just trying to help you move things along."

I blew out a breath. I wasn't typically someone who snapped at my best friend, or anyone else for that matter. And I knew he was just trying to help, but the entire situation had me on edge. "I know."

The alarms blasted from inside, cutting off our conversation.

Fucking great. I had a feeling it was going to be a busy shift. Maybe that was a good thing. It would keep my mind off the blue-eyed, redheaded beauty I couldn't stop thinking about.

Chapter Twenty-Five

LYLA

AFTER DRYING my hands with the towel, I picked up my phone. I still had another half hour before Adam would be back. If he didn't get stuck at the station again. Twenty more minutes, and then I would drain the water from the jacuzzi tub and get out.

I was asleep when he finally came in the night before. I'd stirred awake when he climbed under the covers and pulled me close. And then morning came, and he kissed me breathless again before getting up and heading back to work. Every time I felt his lips, experienced his soft caress against my skin, I was even closer to saying screw it and forgetting about all the ways it could go wrong.

I gasped as I heard the lock on the door disengage. It swung open and Adam appeared. He froze, eyes trained on me, and let the door slam shut behind him.

Shit. I lowered down further into the water. Luckily, the bubbles from the jets hid everything below my shoulders. Our eyes stayed locked, and the surprise in his quickly morphed into pure, intense desire.

God. The way he was looking at me made me want to throw caution to the wind. My breath caught in my throat as he stalked toward the tub and leaned his forearms on the edge. I licked my lips as my gaze traveled over the tattoos that covered his skin. The muscles that stretched up his arms twitched, like he wanted to reach out but was holding back.

"I'm jealous," he rasped. "Looks relaxing."

I swallowed. What would it be like to feel his hands on my bare skin? I squeezed my legs together and he looked down into the water like he sensed the movement.

Before I could consider them, words tumbled from my mouth. "You could join me."

He cocked a brow, and his lips formed a sexy smirk. "If I get in there with you, I might not keep my promise."

"Promise?"

"To take this slow."

He was right. It was a bad idea. Completely opposite of what I thought I wanted. But I was pretty sure my lady parts were taking over at that point. "We could just...talk."

"Yeah. Okay." A throaty chuckle left his lips. "Both of us naked in a hot tub...talking."

My lips parted slightly, forming a sultry pout as I shrugged one shoulder. "Could be fun."

What the heck was going on with me? He studied my face like he didn't know either. But when he stepped back and reached behind to pull his shirt over his head, heat pooled low in my belly. The ink on one arm ran all the way up, over his shoulder, and across his chest. The lines of his muscles were beautifully defined, and I wanted to lick a path along each and every one.

Anticipation tore through my body as his hands went to the waistband of his pants. I'd once imagined him stripping out of his clothes in front of me. Once longed for it. But I'd convinced myself he wasn't interested, firmly allocating him to the colleague box before becoming friends.

But the heat in his eyes as he stared at me, slowly lowering his pants, said he wanted so much more from me. Need and anticipation swirled inside me at the very real idea of us exploring more than "just friends".

He stood to his full height, wearing only his boxer briefs that clung tightly to him. My gaze ran down his toned abs to the deep V that disappeared under the black fabric that outlined his hard cock. The material left very little to the imagination, and it was easy to see he was long and thick.

"I love feeling your eyes on me." His voice dripped with want.

He moved to the edge of the tub and sat down, swinging his legs over the side. I tried to mask the disappointment when I realized he wasn't getting completely naked.

"I plan on keeping my promise." The sexy smirk he sent me confirmed I did a shit job of hiding my dismay.

But somewhere deep down, I was swooning hard. Because even with temptation right in front of him, he still wanted to honor my feelings.

He crossed the tub and came to stand in front of me, placing his hands on either side of me along the back. "But I have no intention of just talking."

He leaned down and claimed my mouth, thrusting his tongue between my lips and quickly turning the kiss needy and desperate. In that moment, I wanted to experience everything with him—his touch. His mouth. His cock deep inside me.

Trailing one hand over my shoulder and down my chest, he cupped my breast and ran his thumb back and forth over my nipple. I arched into his touch, seeking more, and moaned into his mouth. The fingers of his other hand tangled in my messy

AJ RANNEY

bun, tugging my head back and breaking the kiss. His lips skated across my jaw and down the column of my throat.

Pleasure raced through me as he pinched my nipple. "Adam," I purred in response.

Before I knew what he intended to do, he had his hands on my ass and was lifting me out of the water. Pulling me against his body, he spun to settle where I'd just been, sitting with me straddling his lap. His thick, hard cock pressed against me and my chest was on full display for him.

"So beautiful." He ran his hands up my sides, lifting and cradling my breasts. Leaning down, he captured my nipple with his mouth.

"Ohh," I whimpered, reaching up to thread my fingers through his short hair, grasping it tightly. My heart felt like it was about to leap from my chest, my breath escaping in short gasps as he moved to the other side, giving it the same attention.

I rocked against him, seeking friction. Needing so much more. Panting, I moved back and forth over his hard shaft as he continued to lick and suck my nipples.

He pulled back and heat blazed in his eyes as he stared at me. "Jesus, love. That feels amazing." He trailed his fingers down my sides and gripped my hips, stopping me from moving.

I shot him a sexy pout. If it made us both feel good, why was he stopping me from moving?

He chuckled and shook his head. "But if you keep that up, I'm a hundred percent gonna come."

My lips parted slightly with a breathy gasp, loving that I affected him that much.

His fingers dug into the flesh of my ass, keeping me flush against him, but perfectly still. "Will you let me taste you?"

I bit down on my lower lip. The thought of being laid out in front of him completely naked made me nervous. I knew I had a great rack, so the position we were currently in was perfect.

I did my best to be confident in who I was, but I was still a lights-off type of girl. I wasn't small. I didn't have a flat stomach, and my thighs totally touched when I walked. "Do you know how many times I've fantasized about getting my mouth on your pretty little pussy?" He slid one hand down my lower stomach, stopping when his thumb reached my clit. He flicked it and I almost jumped, but he held me firmly in place.

"Adam," I cried out.

"Let me use my tongue to make you come."

How did I say no to that? The desire he aimed at me gave me all the confidence I needed. I nodded and his thumb flicked against me again.

"Need your words, love." The smirk that formed on his face said he was enjoying this.

"Please, Adam." I jerked against his hand. "I want to feel your mouth on me."

He grabbed my ass and stood, holding me against him. Spinning again, he sat me down on the cold tile that surrounded the jacuzzi. I leaned back, my body vibrating with nervous anticipation as he pushed my thighs apart. My core throbbed from his darkened gaze, and he smoothed his hands up my legs, holding them open.

"You're going to taste so good." He lowered his head and buried his face between my legs.

He licked a path from my entrance to my clit, and a whimper caught in my throat as he used his tongue to flick back and forth against the sensitive bundle of nerves. I threaded my fingers tightly in his hair, holding him against me and rocking my hips to the rhythm of his tongue.

"Oh my God," I screamed when he sucked hard.

He paused and looked up at me. "You like that?"

"Yes. Do it again."

He smirked. "I think I like bossy Lyla."

"Good." I sent him my own smirk. "Now do it again."

"As you wish." His mouth covered my pussy, and he sucked hard on my clit.

After a moment, he switched back to flicking it with his

tongue, alternating between the two motions and causing pleasure to build quickly. A throaty moan slipped between my lips
and my core tightened. I thrust up, pressing myself hard against
his mouth. My whole body shook, but he didn't stop, just
continued his assault. The waves of pleasure built, each one
stronger than the last.

"Adam, please." I held his head tight and rocked my hips
against him. "Oh my God," I screamed out as my orgasm over-
took me.

Jesus. I'd never experienced anything like that before. I
slumped back, my body completely spent. He pulled back, and a
tiny gasp left my lips when his tongue licked a slow, gentle path
from my entrance to my clit. He did it two more times, devouring
every drop of my pleasure.

Fucking hell. Who was this guy?

My gaze tracked him as he peppered kisses along my belly and
all the way up my body, until his mouth was close to my ear.

"Just like I thought," he murmured. "Fucking delicious."

I smiled, doing my best to push away any doubts and just
enjoy the moment. He pulled me off the ledge and sat down,
guiding me back to his lap, and I snuggled against his chest as he
held me close.

Suddenly, everything felt so surreal. A large part of me felt like
we'd been together for months. He had become one of the most
important people in my life, and being with him tonight felt so
right. So normal.

And I wanted more. So much more.

Chapter Twenty-Six

LYLA

Tuesday 10:08 a.m.

Izzy: Lyla, how's things going with Adam?

> Me: It's so complicated, and I don't know what to do.

Mia: Complicated how?

> Me: He gave me the best orgasm of my life in the jacuzzi last night but stopped things from going too far because we're supposed to be taking things slow.

Me: But now I don't know if I even want to take things slow.

Me: I want him. Desperately. But I'm scared, and I have no idea how to tell him that.

Izzy: What are you scared of?

Me: What if it doesn't work out?

Mia: I hate to be the one to point out the obvious at the risk of sending you spiraling. But girl, you guys have already crossed that line. There's no going back to being just friends.

Izzy: Mia!

Nicole: She does have a point. Lyla, before you spiral, answer me this... Would you regret not taking a chance on seeing what the two of you could have?

Me: I don't want to go back. I'm just scared of things not working out.

Izzy: Tell him that. He probably feels the same.

Me: I don't know...he seems so confident. So sure about us.

Nicole: Or he just isn't letting the what-ifs overpower how he feels about you.

Izzy: Everyone always has those fears in relationships. How have you dealt with them before?

Me: I haven't. I've never really cared that much if the relationship worked out or not.

Izzy: So why is Adam different?

Me: Because he means so much to me. The thought of not having him in my life literally makes me sick to my stomach.

Izzy: ....

Me: Oh fuck.

Mia: Jesus. Took you long enough.

Nicole: Well, there ya go. Now you need to tell him all that.

Me: Any ideas on how I'm supposed to do that?

Mia: Just get naked. He'll get the idea.

Izzy: Mia!

Nicole: It's not the worst idea.

Me: Ugh. You guys suck.

Chapter Twenty-Seven

ADAM

SMILING AND STIFLING A YAWN, I glanced down at the mess of dark red curls fanned out on my chest. Lyla's leg was draped over mine, her hand tucked under my side. I'd been awake for almost half an hour, trying not to move and wake her. My body had gotten used to waking up before seven each morning over the past three days, so it was no surprise I woke as the sun arose.

A full day off felt like the best kind of luxury, and I was excited about the opportunity to spend the day with Lyla. She'd barely stirred when I got back late after another long shift. Part of me had hoped I would be back early enough to grab dinner with her. And maybe convince her to let me make her come with my tongue again. I had not stopped thinking about it since Monday night. I craved her in a way I'd never craved a woman before.

I held my breath as she stirred slightly. It had to be after seven thirty already, and her physical therapy was at ten. She would want breakfast and coffee before we left. So, as much as I hated to do it, I needed to wake her up shortly.

I ran one hand up and down her back. After a moment, she shifted and groaned.

"I'm not ready to get up," she mumbled. "Can I skip PT and just stay in bed with you?"

Grinning at the visuals my mind conjured up, I swallowed down the urge to tell her yes. Because I fucking loved that idea. But I couldn't say yes. Her physical therapy appointments were important.

Her mom had taken her on Monday, and Dylan had Ethan drive her yesterday. I asked her at one point if she wanted to go get her car. She was cleared to drive, and I thought she might appreciate the little bit of independence that brought her. But she'd quickly said no. I was starting to worry the accident had left her nervous about getting behind the wheel. She seemed completely fine when I was driving, though, so that didn't make a lot of sense. But being a passenger and getting behind the wheel were completely different things.

She shifted again and let out a tiny moan when her pussy rubbed against my leg. I pinched my eyes closed. I was not strong enough to stop this, nor did I want to. But we needed to be quick.

She gasped as I rolled her to her back, smirking at her as I pulled her tank top down to reveal one full, round breast. "We only have a few minutes." I pinched her nipple, rolling it between my fingers, and she arched up. "You gonna be a good girl and come quickly for me?"

With a nod, she bit down hard on her bottom lip. I claimed her mouth and moved my hand lower, trailing under the waistband of her sleep shorts and panties. Damn. She was already soaking wet. I swallowed down her moans as I pushed two digits inside of her and circled her clit with my thumb.

Her breathing sped up as I quickly slid my fingers in and

out. She broke the kiss, throwing her head back, and I trailed my mouth down her neck, sucking hard on the skin there. The need to leave my mark on her, claim her as mine, was overwhelming.

Her inner walls tightened around me, and I curled my fingers, seeking that spot that would send her flying over the edge. "Come for me, love," I murmured against her ear.

She gripped my biceps, digging her nails in, and screamed out as her slick channel pulsed with waves of pleasure. I slowed my movements and peppered kisses along her jaw and down the column of her throat.

"Adam," she said, her voice still heavy with lust.

I raised up on my elbow to look at her. She studied me for a moment, uncertainty swimming in her blue irises. My stomach bottomed out and fear gripped me as I contemplated what the look in her eyes meant.

"I want to make you feel good too."

Her sleepy voice was whisper-quiet and raspy, bringing a myriad of feelings. I closed my eyes briefly as relief hit me. She didn't want to slow down. Or worse, go back to being just friends. My heart wouldn't be able to handle that.

I opened my mouth to respond, mostly to tell her that making her come does make me feel good.

She pressed one finger against my lips and shook her head. "I know we don't have time right now. But next time, I want to watch you come undone as I take you in my mouth."

My cock jumped at the idea, the fact that she was already planning for a next time making me overwhelmingly happy.

But what did it mean? I didn't want to push her for more than she was ready for. And never had I ever wanted any kind of label with a woman, but damn, did I want that with her.

I brushed her curls away from her face and tucked them behind her ear. "I can't wait to feel your lips wrapped around me."

She sighed. "Wish we didn't have to get up."

"Me too, love." I bent and placed a quick kiss on her lips. "But if you want breakfast and coffee, we'd better get a move on."

"Fine," she said with a pout.

I chuckled and rolled off her, climbing out of bed. "Gonna jump in the shower real quick."

She raised up on her elbows, her brows pulling together as her eyes lowered to my hardened length tenting my boxer briefs.

I shot her a smirk. "Don't worry. I'll wait and let you take care of that later." I winked. "But I'm not sure I can leave this room if I don't at least take a cold shower."

"So I guess joining you is out of the question?"

"Fuck, love. Are you trying to kill me today?"

She chuckled with a slight shrug, and I shook my head and trudged toward the bathroom, fighting the urge to say screw physical therapy and have her join me in the shower. On her knees, preferably. Or better yet, straddling my lap on the bench seat and riding my cock.

THE SHOWER HELPED my physical issue, but it did nothing to tame my desire for her. After she got a quick shower and we grabbed a bite to eat, we were on our way to her appointment. I reached over and entwined our hands. She smiled and relaxed back in her seat.

"So what's the plan for after PT?"

"I figured we would grab lunch at some point and then head over to the shelter for the photo shoot."

I slowed the car as we approached a closed intersection. There was a cop directing all traffic to turn right. Lyla stiffened, squeezing my hand slightly. Her chest rose and fell with shallow breaths as her eyes went wide, locked on the scene of the two-car collision.

"Hey." I brushed my thumb over the back of her hand,

needing to draw her attention to me and away from the scene in front of us. "Look at me."

She blinked and turned her head toward me. I took a minute and ran down a quick assessment in my head. How was her breathing? Was she shaking? Could I check her pulse without her realizing what I was doing? At the moment, nothing screamed panic, but the original shallow breathing and wide eyes I noticed still had me concerned.

"You okay?" I finally asked.

She nodded. "Yeah. I'm fine." Her brows pulled together. "Why?"

"Thought maybe the accident upset you."

She yanked her gaze away and shifted in her seat. "Nah. I'm good."

I studied her for another moment, wondering if she was even aware of her reaction. But there was no sign of anything now, so maybe I was just reading too much into it.

But if I wasn't, I'd be there to help her every way I could.

Chapter Twenty-Eight

LYLA

I could still feel Adam's gaze on me. Assessing, studying, speculating—all the things I would do if I was him. But I was fine. Totally fine. I didn't even remember the accident, so how could it affect me? I pushed away my thoughts as we pulled up at the physical therapy office. I knew I'd have to deal with it all eventually, but today wasn't that day.

The session went by quickly and I was happy with my progress. The therapist confirmed I should have no issue going back to work in a week—which half excited me, but also made me a bit nervous. Would the arsonist try coming after me again? At this point he had to know I couldn't ID him. As far as I knew he hadn't been spotted, but I had no clue what that meant for me. For Adam too. How long would I need to hide out here? Would

Adam head back to his apartment eventually? So many unknowns and I was trying my best to not spiral down the rabbit hole.

"So, lunch?" Adam smiled as he drove the car out of the parking lot.

I nodded. "Mexican?"

He chuckled. "I should have guessed."

I tried to stay in the moment, just enjoy being with him, but I couldn't stop my thoughts from circling back to all the reservations I had. Whether I would really be good to go back to work next week. And what things between Adam and I would look like. I was finally confident that I wanted to move forward, but obviously things would be different and need adjusting. In our personal relationship and professional one as well.

VIOLET and I were enjoying our task of helping corral and keep an eye on the cute dogs and adorable kittens between shots, and everything was going well.

Well... almost everything.

I looked back over at Adam and narrowed my eyes as Savannah laughed again, reaching up to tame a stray piece of his hair. Why couldn't she keep her hands to herself? Was she always this flirty with the guys and I'd just never noticed?

"Uh oh." Violet's voice broke through my thoughts. "What did Adam do?"

I tore my gaze away from Adam and Savannah, looking at Violet. "Huh?"

"You're shooting him daggers."

I shook my head, not sure if I wanted to admit who I was really glaring at. "Not him."

She glanced back over at the pair. "Oh." Chuckling, she added, "I guess Seth was right."

"What do you mean?"

"At the Labor Day parade, he thought you guys were more than just friends."

Was it really that obvious to everyone else, and I'd been so blind to it?

Adam looked over at me and smiled. My heart rate ticked up a notch as I took him in. His suspenders fit snug over a tight white T-shirt with his black ink a stark contrast and the adorable puppy in his arms was the perfect vision of sexy and sweet.

His brows slowly scrunched together as he stared back at me. Savannah chose that moment to squeeze his biceps before stepping back to snap the picture. I bit down hard with my back teeth, fighting the urge to go over and smack her.

"Careful. You're going to break a tooth if you keep that up," Violet teased.

If I'd just embraced being with him when he kissed me that night in his apartment, then I wouldn't even be in this predicament. He would be mine and I would be his and everyone would know that. But I didn't plan on letting another night go by without telling him I was ready. That I wanted all of it.

For the rest of the afternoon, I truly tried ignoring Savannah's constant flirting, but I failed miserably. By the time Adam and I were in the car and heading back to the lodge, I was beyond annoyed. I crossed my arms and glared out the window. Maybe I should have just walked up to Adam and kissed him and made it clear to everyone where we stood.

"Are you mad at me for something?" His tone was laced with concern.

I whipped my gaze toward him. "What?"

"You seemed really pissed off during the photo shoot, and you haven't said a word since we got in the car."

"I wasn't mad at you."

"Okay..." The one word held so much skepticism.

I sighed. "Did you not notice Savannah flirting and touching you the whole time?"

His eyes widened as he looked over at me, and a smile broke out on his face.

"Why are you smiling?" I glared at him. Did he like that Savannah fussed over him?

"Because if you're jealous, it means you care," he said with a smirk.

I scoffed. "I'm not—"

He chuckled, cutting off my words, and cocked a brow.

What the hell was I trying to say? Of course, I was jealous. So unbelievably jealous that I wanted to literally claw that woman's eyes out. And he was right. It was because I cared. A lot. But as I thought about what he said, I needed him to understand caring about him was never the issue.

"You're right. I was jealous. I hated watching her flirt with you." I rested my hand on top of his. "But the reason I've been reluctant about this isn't because I don't care. It's because I care so much. You are one of the most important people in my life. Even the thought of losing you breaks my heart into a million pieces."

His smirk faded and he nodded. "I know. I feel the same way."

"You do?" I swallowed.

"Of course." He shifted his hand to join ours together, rubbing his thumb over the back of my hand, sending jolts of electricity up my arm. "But honestly, the thought of never being with you makes me feel just as devastated."

My heart rate picked up, and I couldn't wait another minute to tell him I felt the same. "Well, it's a good thing neither of us will have to find out how that feels."

He glanced over with an eyebrow raised. "What are you saying, love?"

I felt heat creeping up my neck and into my face. He pulled to a stop at a red light, and I locked eyes with him. How did I say I wanted to be his in every way imaginable?

"I'm done second-guessing this." I squeezed his hand. "Because now I can't imagine not being with you."

Chapter Twenty-Nine

ADAM

REACHING OVER, I threaded my fingers through her hair and pulled her to me. I poured all of my devotion and desire for her into the kiss as I slanted my lips over hers. A horn blared and I reluctantly pulled back, accelerating through the intersection.

More than anything, I wanted to pull over and kiss her without being rushed. But the next time I put my lips on her, I didn't want to have to stop.

She shifted in her seat with a tiny giggle, and I glanced over.

A brow rose above one eye. "In a hurry?"

I let off the gas, completely unaware of how fast I was going. Typically, I was always in control, but when it came to her... Sometimes, I felt chaotic.

"Sorry," I said, guilt churned in my gut. If she was having a little bit of PTSD from the accident, she didn't need me driving like a lunatic. "I'll slow down."

She chuckled, squeezing my hand. "I trust you."

The words settled in my chest. I didn't realize how badly I craved that from her. Or in general. Being with someone who allowed me to be me.

"Besides, I'm kind of in a hurry, too."

Teasing weaved through her voice, and I shook my head with a smirk as I pushed the gas down, speeding back up.

I knew these roads far too well. Spending my teen and young adult years driving to and from Zack's had made me as comfortable on them as the roads at home. His parents' house was on the same property as the lodge, and it had been practically a second home to me.

Lyla's finger traced the tattoos on my forearm, sending pinpricks of desire shooting straight to my cock.

"Don't forget your promise to me."

I tried not to react. Tried not to show my disappointment. If she wasn't ready, I would one hundred percent respect that. I would be happy just holding her all night if that was what she wanted. Maybe she would let me bury my face between her legs again.

"You promised next time I could make *you* feel good."

I smiled. Ah, that promise. Although I wouldn't stop her, I wanted her to know that simply being with her made me feel amazing. "Giving you pleasure does make me feel good."

She huffed, crossing her arms with a pout.

"But if it'll make you happy, I'll let you do whatever you want to me."

Her eyes glinted with mischief. "Oh, really? Whatever I want?"

I nodded. Because I really would do anything to make her happy.

We made record time getting back to the lodge and hurried through the lobby to the elevator. As soon as the doors closed, I pulled her to me and pressed my lips to hers. The moment the doors opened, I grabbed her hand, leading her down the hall to our room.

The minute we were inside, we were a tangle of hands and lips. Desperate, passionate, needy. I groaned when her fingers moved under my shirt, brushing over the bare skin of my back. She broke the kiss as she lifted my shirt, and I grabbed the hem behind my neck, pulling it off.

She licked a path up and over my pec, swirling her tongue around my nipple. My hand tightened in her hair, and a feral groan rumbled through my chest. If this was what her mouth felt like on my chest, how the hell was I going to survive her lips on my cock.

Her fingers dropped to the button of my jeans, popping it and lowering the zipper. I stepped back, hastily lowering the pants and kicking them to the side.

A sexy smirk lit her face, and with her hands on my chest, she walked me backward until I was standing in front of one of the large armchairs. She pushed on my chest, and I sat down.

I tipped my chin toward her. "I want you naked if you're gonna get on your knees."

"I—" She suddenly became nervous, wrapping her arms around herself.

I wasn't an idiot. I knew she had some reservations about her body. But there was no way I planned to let her hide from me. She gave in to the moment in the hot tub, letting me lay her out and feast on her, but I wanted her to embrace letting me take my time admiring her body.

Sitting up, I pulled her between my legs, looking up at her. "Please, love. Let me see every inch of your gorgeous body."

Her gaze searched my face, uncertainty still swirling there. She pushed away, stepping back, and for a minute, I wasn't sure if she would do it or not.

Finally, she grabbed the hem of her sweater, lifting it slowly, revealing every delectable curve inch by inch. I smiled and relaxed back into the chair, enjoying the show. Her round tits—confined in a lacy blue bra—drew every ounce of my attention as she removed the shirt over her head, and I licked my lips as she flicked open the clasp nestled between her breasts. Her rosy nipples hardened to points under my gaze and my cock jumped, ready to come out and play.

"You make me feel sexy," she murmured, hooking her thumbs under the waistband of her leggings.

"Because you are sexy." I held her gaze for a moment before trailing it back down her body. "Now, let me see that delicious pussy."

She worked her leggings down her luscious thighs and over her adorable feet, my mouth practically watering as her pants joined the rest of our discarded clothing on the floor. Her fingers teased along the hem of her blue lacy panties and another deep groan rose up in my throat.

"Those too, love." I held onto the arms of the chair to stop myself from getting up and throwing her ass on the bed so I could devour her.

Ever so slowly she slid the fabric down and stepped out of them. Fuck, she was beautiful. I ran my gaze from her full breasts over her soft stomach and the flare of her hips. I wanted to grab her and guide her onto my painfully hard cock. Watch her tits bounce as she rode me. But I made her a promise, and I had no intention of breaking it.

I held my breath as she stepped between my legs and dropped to her knees. This might end up destroying me, but I was one hundred percent ready for it.

She guided my boxer briefs past my hips, freeing my length. Her tiny hand wrapped around the base, and I locked my jaw. I just prayed I didn't embarrass myself and explode in her mouth the minute she took me in. Her blue eyes darkened to almost black as she leaned in and licked up the shaft.

"Fuuuck," I gritted out, throwing my head back. My fingers dug into the arms of the chair as she swirled her tongue over the tip. I looked back down at her, tangling my hand in her hair. "Take me inside."

"Hmm," she hummed, wrapping her lips around the head and slowly pulling me into her warm, wet, sweet little mouth. I couldn't look away. Watching her was almost as pleasurable as the act itself.

She moved back up, her lips grazing along my girth, and I tightened my fingers in her curls as she hollowed out her cheeks. When she got close to the base, I thrust up, encouraging her to take me deeper. And fucking hell, she didn't disappoint, making room in the back of her throat and taking me deeper until my vision blurred.

"Love," I croaked, not sure I could take much more.

"Hmm," she hummed around me again. Her pace picked up, the tip hitting the back of her throat each time she sucked me inside.

"I'm gonna come if you keep this up."

She released me with a pop and looked up at me. Her eyes shone with so much desire and pride it was enthralling. "I want to taste you. To make you lose control."

No way was I telling her no. She opened her mouth, and my cock disappeared inside, taking me deep and swirling her tongue over the tip.

"Fuck," I hissed. "Do that again."

She ran her tongue around my head again until I tugged slightly on her hair, moving her back up my length. She began sliding me in and out, exactly like I wanted her to. I was so close, and her wet lips felt so amazing with each pass, it wouldn't be long before I came. My hips jerked up, matching her rhythm, chasing the precipice. My fingers tightened in her hair, and I grunted as my cock pulsed, emptying into the back of her throat.

I slouched back, my breathing out of control. Fucking hell. That was incredible. I glanced down at her, taking in the sultry smile on her face.

"You can do that whenever you want, love." I reached down

between us, pinching her nipples and rolling them between my fingers. "Now it's my turn. Get that delicious pussy on the bed."

She scrambled to her feet, and I swatted her ass as she turned, moving to the bed. Standing at the foot, I took my time scanning over every inch of her body laid out in front of me. Pink, hard nipples. Her normal creamy skin was tinged with red, and she let her legs fall open slightly as she leaned up on her elbows. It was a perfect peek, but not nearly enough.

I climbed on the bed and pushed her knees farther apart. "You're dripping," I murmured, spreading her wetness with my thumb.

She moaned as I dropped my face to her thighs, arching her back as I kissed a path to her knee and back up. She ignited something needy, almost carnal, in me.

I looked up at her. "I need to taste every inch of you. Then I'm going to fill you with my cock and make you come so many times you lose count."

Her chest rose and fell as her breath came faster. Vulnerability shone in her eyes, but there was more I needed her to know.

"I've wanted you since the day you walked into that class more than six months ago. I've craved this moment with you every single fucking day. This is a dream I never thought was possible."

Her breath halted, then a long exhale followed. She reached out, threading her fingers through my hair. "It's not a dream. This is real, isn't it?"

"So real." My skin felt like it was a million degrees, and my heart pounded out of control.

I couldn't wait another minute to taste her. I dove in, lapping up every drop. Her hands tightened in my hair, almost painfully, but damn did I love it. I licked and sucked, flicking my tongue over her clit as she gasped, her moans getting louder and louder. I groaned at the heady taste of her desire flooding my mouth.

I was so fucking hard, and the moment she squeezed my head between her inner thighs, it sent lust ricocheting through me. I pushed her legs open and raised my face. "Keep your legs spread wide for me, love. Let me ravish this pretty little pussy."

Her gorgeous blue eyes resembled a night sky now, but like the good girl she was, she nodded and let her legs fall open. I growled my approval before diving back between her thighs and feasting on her. Before long, the filthiest words I'd ever heard her mutter were tumbling from her lips. All it did was spur me on, and soon she began to rock her hips, bucking against my face.

She tasted incredible. Better than all my dirty dreams about her, and when she tugged on my hair and cried out, it confirmed it for me. So. Much. Better.

I licked her slowly, giving her a final soft kiss before pulling back and looking down at the gorgeous woman naked before me.

"Fuck, I don't know what I did to deserve you, but I'm never letting you go now."

She gave me a saucy smile. "Sounds a bit stalkery, to be honest."

I crawled up her body, pressing her back into the mattress. "I am definitely obsessed."

I flicked my tongue across one hard nipple before trailing my mouth over to the other one, lavishing attention there until she was moaning again. I gazed down at the redheaded beauty who had quickly become everything my soul didn't know it needed. Heat flooded every damn cell in my body, and the last thing I wanted was anything between us, but we hadn't had that conversation yet. I'd wear a thousand condoms to protect her. Make her feel safe.

"I want nothing more than to take you bare, feel you gripping my cock." I swallowed thickly, realization dawning that I'd never been with anyone without a condom. She would be the first. I'd never been so sure of anyone that I even considered not using one, but I was damn sure that Lyla was my future. And that epiphany spread euphoric bliss through my chest. "But I'll grab a condom if you want me to."

She shook her head. "I trust you, and I'm on birth control."

That part I already knew since the packet of pills had been sitting on my bathroom sink for the last month. "Please, Adam. I want to feel you."

Hovering above her, I lined up my hips flush against her, sinking inside. My brain muddled from the sensation. She was so tight, so hot.

And mine. All mine.

My name was a breathy whisper on her lips. I held back words I wasn't sure she was ready to hear and eased out, then slid back in, letting her feel every inch of me.

Her eyes turn glassy before rolling back into her head. "You feel so good."

It sounded like a confirmation. Like she knew it was going to feel like this. And I had no intention of letting her down.

"Wrap your legs around me. Need to show you just how good it can be."

"Please," she moaned, cinching her legs tightly around my waist and hooking her ankles together.

Slowly, I pulled out, then slammed back in. Once. Twice. On the third time I swiveled my hips, causing the sexiest sounds to tumble from her lips. I needed her to feel the strength of this connection between us. Needed her to lose control for me. I fucked her hard, faster and faster with each thrust.

"Oh God," she moaned over and over again, digging her nails into my shoulders.

Rising up on my knees, I used my thumb to circle her clit. She came hard and fast, her walls squeezing my cock until my vision blurred. But I didn't stop, didn't slow my movements. I wasn't done with her yet.

I pulled out and swatted her ass. "On your hands and knees."

Her wild eyes widened, and I saw a moment of hesitation before she scrambled over and got in position.

I licked my lips as I took in her luscious ass in the air, her pussy still begging to be fucked. I lined myself back up to her entrance and plunged back in. She gasped and I stilled inside her.

The new position allowed me even deeper than before, and damn it felt incredible.

Within minutes, I found a rhythm that had her screaming out my name, begging for release. And I was happy to oblige. Our bodies slapped together and the sound of it propelled me to take her harder and faster. I was desperate to give her another, but my own climax rushed through me, and I couldn't hold back anymore. My whole body seized as I exploded inside of her, and then she cried out again. Almost like my pleasure sent her over the edge too.

My movements slowed, but I didn't stop, allowing her to ride out every wave of her orgasm. Finally, both of us completely spent, we collapsed down onto the mattress. I rolled us to our sides and pulled her close, holding her tight.

And everything clicked into place. She was my forever.

Chapter Thirty

LYLA

MY HEAD RESTING on his chest, I smiled as I swirled my finger in circles over his right pec. Being together for the last twenty-four hours, mostly in this bed, was perfection. The connection I'd felt when we joined was unlike anything I'd experienced before. All the doubts and questions I had about us finally waned, leaving me with only the assurance that we were meant for each other.

We would have another day together before he went on night shifts for three nights. Nerves bubbled up as I thought about my first day back coming up on Thursday.

"Do you think the chief will take you off the shift with me next week?" I was really hoping not, even dreading the possibility. Because there was no doubt I would feel infinitely more comfortable if I was riding with Adam.

"Probably not. But just to be sure, we could wait to disclose our relationship until after you've been back for a few shifts."

I stiffened, not loving that idea. More than anything, I wanted everyone to know he was mine now. But I also really hated the thought of not having him with me on my first shift. I'd officially brushed off my uneasiness as first day back jitters. It was the only thing that made sense.

"But only if that's what you want," he quickly amended. "I'll do whatever makes you most comfortable. Ideally, I really want to ride with you as much as possible when you first go back." He ran his hand soothingly up and down my arm. "I requested we were on the same shifts or riding together on ambo for your first week back."

I smiled, loving the fact that he made sure I would be comfortable and taken care of. I couldn't help but wonder if the chief had questioned it. "Did he not seem suspicious?"

"Nah. I just said having someone ride with you that you're familiar with would be good. He agreed. I think he has you with Kyle once or twice too."

I nodded and nibbled on my bottom lip. "Will you tell the guys?"

He chuckled. "Only if you want me too. Honestly, I'm not sure we'll need to. They'll probably figure it out."

"Why do you say that?"

He kissed the top of my head. "Because after tonight I probably won't be able to stop smiling like an utter fool."

I rolled my eyes, but secretly loved that I made him feel that way.

"But I'll make sure they don't say anything until we're ready," he added.

As much as I wanted everyone to know—including that blonde flirt Savannah and every other single woman in town—I worried that the guys would treat me differently. It already unnerved me that everyone might question if I was ready. Hell, I wasn't even sure I was ready. But I didn't really want to add whispers of a workplace romance on top of that uncertainty.

Not to mention I felt bad asking them to cover for us in front of the chief and Owen.

"Maybe we can wait to tell them too," I said before quickly adding, "You know, officially. Just until after that first week."

I wanted to tell the girls too, but the selfish part of me wanted to revel in this just the two of us for as long as possible.

"Whatever you want."

I tried to read his tone. Did my request upset him?

"Seriously, love. I'm good with whatever will make your first few shifts back the easiest for you."

I sighed and relaxed back into his hold.

"Do you want to finish our game of *Magic*?" he asked.

"Not yet." Snuggling deeper into his side, I let my eyes drift shut.

Being in his arms was the second-best thing. Feeling him move inside me was the first.

But literally every experience with him was the best.

Chapter Thirty-One

LYLA

THE HEAT FELT great on my skin as I stepped down into the water. My foot slipped on the last step and I caught myself before I fell back on my ass. A mix of gasps and chuckles erupted from the girls and I sighed, taking the seat next to Mia. Izzy and Nicole sat across from us in the large, rectangular-shaped hot tub that shared the pool area of The Lodge. Adam was working the night shift, and when Nicole had texted earlier asking if we could all get together, I invited them to come out here and enjoy the pool and hot tub with me.

"This is the perfect girls' night idea," Izzy said with a smile.

"Yeah, I'm jealous." Nicole pouted. "Wish I had access to this every night."

She did realize the only reason I was holed up here was

because an arsonist came after me, right? I shot her a snarky smirk. "Oh, it's easy. Just get yourself a stalker who wants to kill you."

Nicole rolled her eyes and waved me off. "Stop being so dramatic."

I laughed and lifted my shoulders in a slight shrug. "I am who I am." Although, was I actually being dramatic? Or did they just not fully understand how affected I was by it all?

"Or..." Izzy said with a smirk, pointing between Nicole and Mia, "One of you can date the owner's son. Then we can have hot tub nights here all the time."

"Definitely won't be me." Mia rolled her eyes, pursing her lips. "He's so freaking annoying."

"I think he's hot." Nicole fanned herself. And she called me the dramatic one?

"Maybe I can have Logan set up a double date," Izzy offered.

Excited at the idea, I bounced a little in my seat. I sensed Mia tense next to me. Hmm. Maybe she didn't find him as annoying as she said she did.

Izzy aimed a knowing grin at me. "You're being awfully smiley."

I raised a brow. "Really?" I didn't need a mirror to know my cheeks were flushing.

"Yes." Nicole chimed in. "Does it have anything to do with your sexy firefighter?"

I hesitated, the words on the tip of my tongue. Adam's face flickered through my mind, along with the agreement we'd made —keep it quiet at work. But these weren't work people. These were *my* people.

"Okay," I said, lowering my voice even though no one else was around. "You have to promise not to tell anyone."

"I promise," Nicole and Izzy echoed excitedly, leaning forward and waiting for the details.

I raised a brow at Mia and she rolled her eyes.

"Oh, for the love of God," she grumbled. "Yeah, yeah, I promise. Just get on with it."

I took a steady breath. "Adam and I... we're together. Like, officially."

There was a half-second of silence before all three of them smiled knowingly.

"I knew it," Izzy proclaimed.

"Spill all the juicy details." Nicole waggled her brows suggestively. "I need to live vicariously through you."

"Did you take my advice and get naked?" Mia asked.

"Pretty much." I chuckled. "We don't want anyone at work to know yet, so please—seriously—don't say anything. We want to make sure we can still ride together for my first week back."

"Of course," Izzy said and Nicole nodded her agreement.

Mia's smile faded and she studied me before asking, "You go back in a few days, right?"

The question landed heavier than I expected it to. The excitement faded around us, replaced by something cautious.

"Yeah," I said, forcing a shrug. "In a few days."

Izzy tilted her head. "How are you feeling about that? After... everything."

I waved a hand, like I could brush the memory away. "I'm good. Really. Just a little jittery, I guess. But once I'm there and back into the swing of things, I'll be fine."

The words sounded practiced even to my own ears. But I hoped if I said it enough the uneasiness would begin to diminish.

They didn't say anything right away. Instead, Izzy glanced at Nicole, Nicole looked at Mia, and Mia looked back at me. It was subtle, but I caught it—the shared look, the unspoken doubt.

"Okay," Nicole said carefully. "If you say so."

"Just... don't push yourself," Mia added.

I smiled, hoping it looked convincing. "I won't."

The quiet concern lingered between us until Izzy not so subtly changed the topic to her wedding planning. I tuned in to her discussion of centerpieces as I tried to quell the nervous feeling that kept trying to bubble up, convincing myself it was all going to be okay.

Chapter Thirty-Two

ADAM

THREE NIGHT SHIFTS in a row and I was looking forward to holding Lyla in my arms again. Inhaling her sweet scent and caressing her soft skin as I slowly moved in and out of her. Holding her and weaving my fingers through her hair as she fell asleep against me. I just needed to get through a few more hours, then we would have twenty-four hours together before her first day back.

I smiled thinking of the last few days together. We'd spent them sitting by the fire outside, playing *Magic*, taking her to her physical therapy appointments, and getting lost in each other every chance we got.

"Dude." Zack's voice broke through my thoughts.

I glanced over at him as we made our way to the front door of the house we were called to, waiting for Jay to gain entry from the back and let us in. This house was a frequent call and Jay volunteered for the task of getting inside this time. Zack narrowed his eyes on me.

"What?" Did I tune out something he was saying?

"We were woken up to a call for another lift assist and you're smiling."

I cocked a brow. "Would you prefer we be walking into a fire right now?"

His lips slowly lifted into a smirk. "Yeah, kinda."

I shook my head. Somehow, that reply didn't surprise me. Zack wasn't good with idle time or tasks. He lived for the adrenaline high. Always had.

All of us did to an extent. I just never minded the more mundane, simple tasks that came with the job. It was probably why I enjoyed EMT shifts just as much. Helping people was what I lived for. Saving lives, and even the small things that I knew in some way made a difference. I didn't always need to run into burning buildings or rappel down cliffs to get a surge of adrenaline. Risking my life came with the job, but it wasn't the part I loved about it.

His forehead wrinkled as he studied me. I wished I could admit the real reason I was smiling. But I told Lyla I wouldn't tell the guys yet, and there was no way I would betray her trust. I had already told Zack last week that we were easing into things and taking it slow, and even though I trusted him to not say anything, I still didn't want to break my promise.

"How's things going with Lyla?"

Dammit. I searched for what to say. "Good."

Luckily the door swung open, and we followed Jay through the house, putting that entire conversation on hold. Hopefully for another few days, although I'd be lucky and grateful for a few more hours.

After helping the elderly man up off the floor and confirming he wasn't injured, we headed back to the truck. Jay climbed up front while Zack and I got into the back.

"How much longer do you two plan to stay at the lodge?" Zack asked.

I sighed. I'd thought about this issue several times in the last couple of days. The last thing I wanted to do was stress Lyla out right before her first shift back, but I knew I needed to bring up moving back to my apartment. She seemed perfectly content at the lodge, but it couldn't be a permanent thing. Eventually we would have to get back to normal life.

What could be a permanent thing, though, was her with me in my apartment.

"We haven't talked about it yet."

"Probably need to figure that out soon. With both of you back on regular shifts, she's going to need her car. And you probably don't want to be thirty minutes away forever."

"Yeah, I know." I let out a breath as a call came through the radio. Active fire. I sent Zack a glare. "Happy now?"

He chuckled and grinned at me in response.

Asshole.

Chapter Thirty-Three

LYLA

MY HEART RATE picked up as I stared into the back of the ambo, trying and failing to shake off the nervous feeling that flooded me. I breathed in through my nose and out through my mouth. Once... Twice...

"I can do this," I whispered. It was just like riding a bike.

I climbed up into the back, a sudden memory hitting me of being in the back with the elderly man who had chest pain and trouble breathing. I had eased the worry in his eyes with a smile.

My hand shot out, and I leaned against the side with a gasp. I forced all thoughts of that day a month ago to the back of my mind. I needed to pull my shit together. Now was not the time to try to remember.

I started the process of inspecting the rig. Adam and I had

already gotten a report from the outgoing shift, and he was checking the vehicle, putting me in charge of making sure everything was good to go for our first call. I didn't want to let him down. Or any of the crew. And I didn't want the chief or Owen to think I wasn't capable.

Supplies restocked. Check.

Equipment in working order. Check.

Adam appeared at the large open doors, studying me with a concerned expression on his face. "You good?"

I squared my shoulders, willing confidence into my tone. "Yep. Totally good."

He scrutinized me with those piercing dark eyes of his and I sent him a smile. One that I hoped exuded more conviction than I felt. All I needed was a simple call. One call to get back into the swing of things and I'd be good. It was like the night before the first day of school. Every year had been the same deal, but it didn't stop me from being nervous about it. But once I was there, the nerves usually faded quickly.

That was all it was. Just first-day jitters.

The ear-piercing alarms blasted through the bay, and I froze, listening for the radio to crackle to life. The dispatcher relayed the information about an adult male who had an allergic reaction, self-administered an EpiPen, and needed transport to the hospital.

Relieved that it seemed like it was such a simple, routine call, my shoulders relaxed and I shot Adam a smile. "Let's go."

A few more easy calls later, and I felt good. Most of my nerves had faded and I felt almost normal. I scanned the shelves in the small, enclosed alcove that housed all of our extra supplies. I was on the hunt for disinfectant wipes, gloves, and another book of report sheets, wanting to have extras of those things stocked in the ambo.

Glancing over my shoulder, I noticed Adam standing in the archway, leaning one shoulder against the frame. His lips lifted into a sexy smirk as he closed the distance. My breath caught as I turned slightly and stepped back, pressing my back against the wall. With one forearm pressed against the wall near my head, he brought his other hand up and tangled his fingers in my hair.

His gaze darkened to almost black as it locked on my lips, making his intentions perfectly clear. Heat pooled low in my belly as he leaned down, and I gripped the fabric of his uniform, holding him tightly as he explored my mouth. He tasted like coffee and peppermint.

We were lost in each other until the sound of Zack's voice hit my ears. I broke the kiss and pushed Adam away, spinning around and frantically pretending to search the shelves. For what, I couldn't even remember. My brain felt like utter mush at the moment. I rolled my eyes at Adam's chuckle. He would totally find this funny.

"There you are," Zack said. "Oh, and look at that. Lyla too. What a coinkidink."

My face heated to a degree I didn't even know it could achieve.

"What's up?" Adam responded with a sly tone in his voice.

If I wasn't a hundred percent sure spinning around to glare at him would give me away, I would have.

"We're going for a grocery run. Did you two want to come?" Zack paused before adding, "Or you can give us a list of what you need. You know, in case you had things you needed to take care of here."

I wanted to throttle him. Like legit. But I took a deep breath and forced a smile before spinning to face him. His smirk definitely said he knew.

"We'll go." I ignored Adam's raised brow and continued, "I could use a few things."

I brushed past them and headed straight for the rig. Adam and I would follow them just in case a call came through. But I didn't even make it that far before the alarms overhead were blaring. My body stiffened as I listened to the dispatcher give the details of the car accident. Two people trapped with rollover. One car leaking fluid. Multiple injuries.

My stomach revolted, but I didn't have time for nerves right now. I needed to focus on my job.

We loaded up and Adam glanced over at me. "You good?"

I nodded. "Yeah."

"Just follow my lead and you'll be fine."

This would be my first serious call since my shift started. It was now or never.

We pulled up to the scene and I reached for the door handle. My hand shook as I grabbed it, and for a minute I wondered if I could do this. But did I have a choice? These people were depending on me.

A few steps on wobbly feet toward the scene and my heart rate took off at a sprint. I froze as memories of that day assaulted me.

I smiled down at the older man. His eyes were as wide as saucers as he stared at me, inhaling the oxygen I had him hooked up to and squeezing my arm tightly. You could tell he was in good health, and this was not on his bingo card. His vitals were good, but that didn't mean anything. His symptoms could be warning signs of an impending heart attack.

Suddenly, the ambulance swerved and jolted. Instinctively my arm shot out to provide myself additional balance, but just then I flew hard against the wall as the ambulance tipped to the side. Fear gripped me as pain radiated up my arm and my head throbbed from the impact.

Pain. So much pain. Then wetness coated my face and my vision went dark.

Chapter Thirty-Four

ADAM

I STOPPED and glanced back at Lyla, sensing something was wrong. She stood frozen in place, eyes locked on the scene of the accident in front of us. I closed the distance and came to stand in front of her.

"Hey." I cupped her face with my hands. "What's wrong, love?"

She barely acknowledged my touch. She was somewhere else, not here with me.

Fuck. I quickly assessed her, already knowing the telltale signs I'd find. Her breaths came fast and I could feel her shaking under my hands. I moved one hand down to the pulse in her neck, feeling it beating wildly. I needed her to come back to me. My heart screamed that she needed to be my priority, but my brain knew my attention was being pulled in multiple directions, and that wouldn't help anyone. Not Lyla, not the people in the wreck, and not my fellow responders. All my training felt useless at that moment, and that scared the crap out of me.

Just then, a second ambulance pulled up and Kyle hopped out. As a paramedic, he was able to pick up shifts at other stations throughout the county. They were always in shorter supply, and it was important to have paramedic units available throughout the area at all times. This kind of call would likely need that extra support. Some of the tension eased from my shoulders, feeling grateful he was there and could take lead until I could make sure Lyla was good. With multiple victims, I would still be needed though.

Kyle took one look at us and his lips formed a tight line. He tipped his chin toward Lyla. "That's definitely familiar." Former military, he battled with his own PTSD. The empathy that shone in his eyes confirmed what I had already suspected was happening with Lyla.

"Can you guys take lead? I'll be there in a minute." I had no idea how I was going to pull her out, but I had to try. I'd do anything to stop her from feeling pain, or fear, or sorrow.

Kyle shot me a single clipped nod before walking away.

I pulled Lyla to me, wrapping my arms around her. "You're safe, love. I'm here. Breathe with me. Inhale." I counted to four in my head. "Hold it." And then seven seconds. "Slowly let it out." I went through it again. "Feel my heartbeat?"

She nodded slightly and relief flooded me. Wetness soaked my shirt and her arms came around my back, giving me hope that she would be okay. Together we could get through this.

Owen strode toward us, brows pinched tightly together. "What's going on?"

Lyla stiffened in my arms, but I held her tightly in place. "She's having a panic attack."

He glanced at the accident and then back at me. "Did you know this might be a problem?"

I couldn't say no. I had this concern last week when I drove her to physical therapy. "I thought she was handling it." At least I could say that with confidence.

His eyes narrowed on me, and he crossed his arms. "She'll need to be cleared before she can ride again." His gaze softened and he waved to the ambulance. "Put her in the back of the bus with some oxygen."

He turned and hurried back toward the call. I wasn't looking forward to finishing the conversation with him later, but I couldn't think about that at the moment.

Lyla continued to shake in my arms until she leaned back to look up at me. "You have to go help," she sniffled, her voice still shaky.

"Yeah, I know." I let out a heavy sigh, my insides still turning with worry. "Just give me a min."

I held her against my chest, letting myself finally embrace the fear of possibly losing her once again, except this time in a way I was not equipped to deal with. If she was broken and bruised I knew what to do. But this? I felt completely and utterly powerless to do anything.

Funny thing was, I probably needed this moment of holding her and comfort more than she did. To ground myself again and remind me that she was here. She was going to be okay. And I would help her get through it.

Chapter Thirty-Five

LYLA

I SET the phone down on the table and let out a sigh. Kyle had given me the name of the therapist he saw, who specifically deals with PTSD. He'd explained that he still does therapy sessions from time to time, especially after losing a patient since that was a trigger for him.

I'd just made my first appointment.

Why didn't I realize I was struggling? Did I just blindly ignore it? Kyle told me not to beat myself up, but shouldn't I have recognized the problem?

Adam appeared in the doorway of the small conference room. After recovering from my panic attack and returning to the station, I didn't want to be alone. More than that, I wanted to be near Adam. He made me feel safe. Seen and not judged. So, although I couldn't stay on shift, after I showered and changed, I decided to hang around the station for the rest of the day until Adam was off.

"You ready to go?" Concern and almost something like guilt swirled in Adam's irises as he approached me.

I'd overheard him earlier telling Zack that he should have known. That he should have done something. But it wasn't his fault. If I wasn't able to recognize what was going on, how could I have expected him to?

I nodded and stood, walking toward him. He opened his arms, and I melted into his embrace, inhaling his fresh, clean scent. "Don't blame yourself," I whispered, letting the beat of his heart ground me.

"One of the things I love about us is that I can always tell how you're feeling or what you need." He let out a deep sigh. "Except when it mattered the most."

"But I wasn't even sure how I was feeling or what I needed." I hugged him tight. "And you were there to help me through it and bring me back. You knew exactly what I needed."

He pulled back, cupping my face in his hands. "I'll always be there for you." His thumbs brushed along my cheeks and his gaze was like a soft caress as he stared at me. "I love you, Lyla."

My lips parted on an inaudible gasp, but his declaration didn't feel that surprising. Deep down. I knew it... and I felt the same. "I love you, too."

His lips were warm and soft as they brushed tenderly against mine. My body relaxed, warmth and peace enveloping me. He broke the kiss, and after tucking me into his side, we walked toward the back of the building and out to the car.

He held my hand tightly as he drove the car toward the lodge. I probably needed to rip the Band-Aid off and go get my car. That should have been my first clue something wasn't right—when I had no interest in getting behind the wheel of a car.

"You're calm." His words were barely a whisper.

I glanced over, tilting my head. I wasn't sure how to respond.

He looked at me with a slight sigh. "You're not at all anxious when we're in the car together."

I stared out the windshield at the road as he took the curves up the mountain with precision and ease. Did PTSD conform to a distinct set of rules? Or could it be triggered by random but specific stimuli. Adam was trying to make sense of it all, and I not only understood why he was, but I appreciated it too. I really didn't have the answers either. But there was one thing I could offer.

"You make me feel safe." I looked back over at him. "And I don't worry because I'm confident you're paying attention, that you have complete control of the car."

I wasn't worried when he was driving the ambulance either. I just knew. I trusted him.

He squeezed my hand before bringing it to his mouth and pressing his lips to my knuckles, sending zaps of pleasure shooting up my arm. I shifted in my seat as my mind started to imagine his mouth on other parts of my body.

"Did you want to grab something to eat before we head to our room?" he asked, startling me out of my thoughts.

"Yeah, I guess we probably should."

As much as I wanted to head straight to the room and let him hold me, touch me, get lost in the feeling of being with him, neither of us had eaten since lunch. And even then, I'd barely had an appetite. Hopefully a quiet dinner, just the two of us, was exactly what I needed.

BEING with Adam always made things better. No matter what we were doing. I smiled, pulling my hair to one side and twisting my curls into a braid. He'd ordered us a piece of the molten chocolate lava cake, bringing up the fact that I kept salivating over it every time we came, but never ordered it. I didn't need the extra carbs and sugar, but after the day I'd had, I wasn't going to say no.

I finished brushing my teeth and took one final look in the mirror. The cotton sleep tank hugged my breasts and cut low between them. Paired with the short sleep shorts, they were the sexiest pair of pajamas I'd packed.

I exited the bathroom and stopped short, gasping at what Adam had done. He sat in the middle of the mattress that he had placed on the floor in front of the now roaring fireplace, propping the cushions and pillows up against the sofa to act as a headboard. I scanned the room. The lights were off, but Adam had arranged tealight candles everywhere.

Emotions flooded me. I'd never had anyone do something so sweet and romantic for me before. But I couldn't help giggling, thinking it would be my luck if they activated the fire alarms. Zack would never let us live it down.

"I had this planned for after your first day back, and I think you could use it even more after today." He spread his legs wide and patted the mattress in front of him. "Come here, love. I have something else for you."

I raised a brow. I hoped he was talking about his mouth or his cock.

"Not that." He chuckled darkly. "At least not yet."

I sent him a pout as I scampered toward him and onto the mattress, sitting between his legs and settling my back against his warm, solid chest. He grabbed the hem of my shirt, lifting it up and over my head. My bare skin broke out with goose bumps, but the hot air from the fire soothed it. After picking up the bottle of massage cream from the blanket next to us, he put some in his large palms, spreading it over my shoulders and down my back before reaching around and rubbing some along my chest.

I sighed as he began kneading my tight shoulder muscles. "No one's ever done anything like this for me before."

"I will never stop showing you how you deserve to be treated."

Warmth spread through my chest at his words and the

meaning behind them. His hands slid down my arms and then back up, leaving a wake of sensations along my skin.

Sucking in a deep breath, I focused on the feel of his hands and not the ache between my thighs. His thumbs found a spot just under my shoulder blades and I almost drew blood as I bit down hard on my lip to hold in the moan that wanted to slip out. Adam's hands were magic as they worked over the muscles that lined my spine and then glided back up before repeating the pattern.

Between the fire that burned bright, casting the room in a shadowy glow, and the soft flicker of the candles all around us, this was by far the most romantic moment of my life. He pulled me against his chest, massaging the muscles around my collarbones. The moan finally tumbled from my lips when he inched lower, stroking and teasing my breasts.

"Adam," I whimpered, arching my back.

"Shh," His warm breath skated across my ear, and he moved his hands back up over my clavicles. "Relax."

"Kinda hard to do that when you're driving me wild."

He nipped at my ear. "I'm just getting started."

He hadn't even touched me where I needed it the most, but I was already wet and throbbing for him. He flattened his palms and dragged them down over my nipples, causing a bolt of intense pleasure to shoot straight to my core. I dug my fingers into his knees as he did it again and again. My breath came in short gasps as he lavished attention on each breast.

"Spread your legs, love. Drape them over mine."

Another tremor tore through me as I obeyed his command, anticipating the moment he realized I wasn't wearing any underwear. He smoothed one hand down my stomach and over the fabric of my sleep shorts, applying pressure and rubbing back and forth while continuing to massage my chest with his other hand.

"Please," I begged. "I can't take anymore. I need you to touch me."

"Where?" The deep timbre of his voice egged on my desperation. "Show me."

Being with him was such a different experience than I'd ever had. He constantly pushed me out of my comfort zone, and I loved it. He made me feel sexy and desired.

Needed. Craved.

I embraced the feeling, letting it push me further. I draped my fingers over his and moved them lower, brushing the sleep shorts to the side and trailing them through my wetness.

He nipped at my ear. "You were planning to go to sleep like this?"

I shook my head, continuing to tease my entrance with our entwined hands. "I wasn't planning to sleep."

"Such a naughty girl." He slid two fingers deep inside me. "Is this what you needed?" he asked, gliding back out.

"Yes." I applied pressure to his knuckles, pushing him back in.

"So needy," he rumbled, diving in without another warning, pulling the air from my lungs. The hunger in his voice was almost feral, and with the way he curled his fingers, hitting that spot that made me see flashes of white, my hips moved of their own accord, rocking to meet his strokes. Blood pounded through my veins, and every beat of my heart was faster than the one before.

Pressing back into him and lifting my hips off the floor, my moans echoed around us. He plunged into me harder. Twisting, curling, and using his palm to rub against my clit. He held nothing back, as it was obvious he had one goal in mind—to completely and utterly destroy me. And damn did I want him to.

"Adam," I hissed as my core tightened.

He continued to fuck me with his hand, drawing out each wave of my orgasm. My body quivered one last time before I melted into his hold, completely spent.

I lay there in his arms, the light of the fire bouncing off the walls, as he peppered kisses along the shell of my ear and down the column of my throat.

He shifted out from behind me, laying me down and peeling

away my shorts. "Need to feel you clenching around me like you did my fingers." He kissed his way back up my body, making my skin tingle in his wake.

His mouth met mine, our lips soft and the kiss unhurried, both of us putting everything we were feeling into it. My need to connect with him overwhelmed me, and I gripped the back of his head, holding him tightly to me. I whimpered my disappointment when he pulled away, but it was immediately replaced with anticipation as he shimmied out of his boxer briefs.

Thank God. Because I desperately needed him. More than I'd ever needed anything.

He climbed back on top of me, positioning himself between my legs and tenderly brushing the hair off my face. His lips descended on mine, and with every swipe of his tongue, I was reminded that this man loved me. Adored me. Hungered for me. Just like I did him.

The feelings settled deep inside me, and I held him tight as he lined up the tip of his cock with my entrance and slowly pushed forward.

Simultaneously, we moaned from the sensation. His gaze held mine with such intensity and longing as he began to move, the words weren't even necessary. But a need to tell him anyway burned until I couldn't stop myself.

"I love you," I whispered, running the tips of my fingers along his back.

He smiled down at me. "Jesus, love. Hearing you say those words to me..." He visibly swallowed, vulnerability staring back at me. "You can't imagine how happy it makes me."

I could imagine, because hearing them from him earlier had the same effect on me.

"I love you so much that I wish I could put it into words."

I smiled, digging my nails into his ass. "Then show me instead."

His lips lifted into that sexy smirk of his and I trembled,

knowing what that look meant. Knowing he would pour everything he had into pleasing me. Obliterating me all over again.

He moved slowly at first, his gaze never straying from mine, instead boring into me as our bodies slid together in perfect harmony. He reached down and lifted my thigh over his hip, the angle allowing him to plunge deeper and faster. Our desire for each other quickly ramped up as I clawed at his back, feeling like he was claiming me with each thrust.

I moved my hips, matching his rhythm as we collided again and again, somewhere between fucking and making love. My belly seized, and I screamed out in pleasure seconds before I felt him tighten under my touch. He dug his fingers into my thigh, holding me tight as he bucked furiously into me. My body convulsed, each spasm feeling stronger than the one before, and I arched up into him. My pussy felt so full. I never wanted this feeling to end.

He grunted, slamming into me one last time and emptying himself deep inside me. His weight collapsed down onto me and I didn't even care that I couldn't breathe. Because holding him like this, being connected to him like this, was worth it.

His lips brushed against the column of my throat before he shifted, sliding out of me. We both let out a sigh at the loss of connection, and he rolled onto his back, bringing me with him so I was tucked into his side.

I wanted to stay in the moment with him. Not allow my mind to wander back to today and everything that transpired. But as a flood of emotions rushed through me, I couldn't stop myself from feeling it all. A single tear slipped down my cheek, landing on his chest.

He lifted my chin to look at him. "What's wrong, my love?"

My love. Oh my God. He was calling me *his* love this entire time. How the hell was I so blind? To all of it. Tears fell more freely now, and concern etched his features.

Quickly, I shook my head. "Nothing's wrong. That was amazing. And after today, I guess..." How the hell did I explain female emotions? I wasn't sure I truly understood them.

"I broke the dam you built to hold yourself together?" he inquired, obviously understanding my feelings better than I did.

I chuckled, laying my head back on his chest. "Exactly."

"Good." He tightened his hold on me. "I don't ever want anything else between us. No more dams."

I took in a shaky breath. "What if I don't get over this?"

"You will." He pressed his lips to the top of my head. "We'll do it together." He was quiet then, almost like he wanted to say more.

"I feel like there's something you're not saying. Nothing between us, remember? That goes both ways."

He sighed. "I'm not sure if you're ready to hear it." He paused before adding, "I think we should move back to my apartment." I stiffened, but he quickly continued. "In order to feel safe at work, you have to feel safe at home. But being here is just a temporary safe feeling. Isn't it? And we can't hide out here forever."

He had a point that I couldn't argue with. Reluctantly, I nodded. Maybe that would be the logical first move, but in reality... "I can probably move back to my apartment at this point."

His hold on me tightened. "No."

"I don't need help anymore, and like you said—"

"You're right, you don't *need* to stay with me anymore. But I *want* you there. I want to come home every night to you."

I popped up on my elbow, staring at him in surprise. Was he saying what I thought he was?

He chuckled like he could read my mind. "We've pretty much been living together for over a month now."

"Well... yeah. But..." It wasn't that I didn't want that, but there were other things to consider. "I'm committed to splitting the apartment with Mia until March."

He smiled. "That's fine. I just want you in my bed every night and every morning."

I rolled my eyes. He was ridiculous. I laid my head back down on his chest with a smile on my face. I couldn't even argue with him, because at the end of the day, that was what I wanted too.

Chapter Thirty-Six

LYLA

AFTER A HANDFUL of sessions with the therapist over the week following my breakdown, I was cleared to come back to work. I still had to continue seeing her for at least the next six weeks, but I planned to keep maintenance appointments with her even after the six weeks were up. Understanding what caused my anxiety, talking through it and what I needed to do to keep myself calm, I felt confident in my ability again.

The sessions ended up being eye-opening on many levels. We didn't just start with the accident, instead we revisited things from my childhood and early adult years. Things I had unconsciously pushed down and never really dealt with. Like the girl from my biology class sophomore year of high school who died in a car accident. I'd declined the counseling the school offered because I didn't know her that well and thought it was silly to grieve someone I hardly knew. But the minute we touched on it, I could feel the way my body tensed and my heart rate accelerated. Overall, the sessions made me realize I had to start actually processing things, not just tamping them down or brushing them aside.

Now, armed with medication, mindfulness and breathing techniques, and finally some exposure therapy to work through the visceral reactions, I had all the tools needed to conquer my demons.

The Mayday alert came through my radio, and I froze, staring up at the house fully engulfed in fire.

I glanced over at Adam, who was riding with me again. After the incident, we moved back to Adam's apartment and disclosed our relationship to the chief. Of course he wasn't surprised, nor were any of the guys. However, we were pleasantly surprised when we were paired together for a few shifts in the next week. The chief explained that with one EMT on bereavement leave and another one on vacation, he was short-staffed and didn't really have a choice. But he also trusted us to be able to do our jobs, be professional. That meant a lot to both of us, and there was no way we would betray that trust either.

Adam stood with crossed arms and a look of pure rage on his face as he stared at the house. He was so pissed that we were here because of the arsonist once again. Jay's voice came through the radio, explaining that Seth had fallen through the floor while they were doing their primary search. The color drained from Adam's face as Jay relayed back that he was not sure of Seth's status.

Owen screamed out commands to the crew and the set of volunteers who had just shown up, sending in two teams of two to assist. He also radioed dispatch requesting a paramedic unit, just in case Seth needed to be intubated or needed other advanced life support Adam and I couldn't provide as EMTs.

We worked quickly to pull the stretcher out and get it as close to the front entrance as we could, ready to take over when they brought him out. My stomach turned. There was always that possibility that one day someone wouldn't make it out.

No. Not today. We were not losing one of our own. I felt sick just thinking about his girlfriend, Violet, receiving that kind of news.

The minute Logan and Jay appeared, carrying Seth, Adam rushed forward. A couple of volunteers followed, and I breathed a sigh of relief that everyone was out.

As soon as we had Seth settled on the stretcher, Adam and I began our assessment.

"Is he breathing?" Jay choked out, his voice strained, followed by a cough with a slight wheezing sound accompanying it.

"Yeah," I answered, meeting Adam's gaze, a silent conversation happening between us. Jay needed to be checked out too.

"You good?" Adam asked me.

I nodded, getting the oxygen mask secured in place on Seth's face.

Adam turned toward Jay. "Need to take a listen, man."

Jay pulled his shoulders back and scowled at Adam. "I'm fine. Focus on Seth."

"Mitchell," Owen yelled.

Jay's head snapped in that direction. Owen's stern no-nonsense stare said all he needed to.

"Fucking hell." Jay pulled off his gloves with a huff and brushed past Adam. "Let's get this over with."

I sighed. These men were the most stubborn group of guys I'd ever met.

Less than five minutes later, Jay stomped away—seemingly getting a clean bill of health—and Adam appeared next to me, bumping my shoulder and sending me a comforting smile.

I glanced over at him. Tensing up, he squinted into the distance. Following his gaze, I stiffened as I saw a figure wearing a green hoodie lingering at the tree line. Fear mixed with anger buzzed through my body.

Before I could even mutter a word, Adam took off running that way.

"Wait," I yelled. What the hell was he thinking? I knew he was pissed and sick of dealing with this guy, but he couldn't just leave a scene to chase after a possibly dangerous criminal.

And what was I supposed to do? I couldn't leave Seth and go after him. I glanced around, wishing the second ambulance would show up already.

Shock infiltrated my thoughts, my emotions heightening my distress. Adam was always so levelheaded. He was the last one of these guys I'd expect to do that. Just like the rest of us, he was angry and beyond frustrated that we were still dealing with the arsonist. But his impulsive decision was reckless. What if he got hurt? Or worse. My heart beat faster at that thought.

Zack jogged over, brows pulling together as he stared after Adam. "Where's he going?"

"Adam took off after someone in a green hoodie." The words tumbled quickly from my mouth.

Zack's eyes widened. "Jesus Christ. We don't have time for this. I need to put out a fire, not save his ass from being stupid." And then he was gone too, sprinting after Adam.

Pinching my eyes closed, I used one of the breathing techniques my therapist taught me to calm my mind and body and help stop myself from spiraling. After a moment, I opened my eyes and looked around. Everyone else was busy, still working the fire. But someone needed to update Dylan. I pulled out my phone and shot off a quick text, updating him not only about the arsonist and the two knuckleheads who gave chase, but also about Seth. That way he could let Violet know and fill in any details she hadn't already heard.

Focusing back on Seth, I checked his vitals again. The sound of sirens approaching registered, and I whispered, "Thank God."

The paramedic unit pulled up a moment later, and after I updated the pair, they loaded Seth into the back and drove off to the hospital.

I turned just in time to see Zack trudging back toward me. His lips formed a tight line. "Lost him."

I stood there, staring blankly at the tree line, praying Adam would appear.

Dylan pulled up, and I didn't even have a chance to fully update him before gunshots rang out in the distance. They were coming from the woods.

No. This was not happening. My heart plummeted, and if I didn't already have adrenaline coursing heavily through my body, I probably would have collapsed to the ground.

Please don't let him be shot. I wrapped my arms around my middle, a knot forming in the pit of my stomach. I couldn't lose him.

Not after we'd just found our way to each other and what we both truly wanted.

Chapter Thirty-Seven

ADAM

THE BARK of the tree I leaned against felt rough on my back, but the pain just below my ribs grabbed most of my attention. I gasped for air, sinking down to the ground, and pressed firmly against my side. Deep breaths, I reminded myself.

My vision blurred.

Do not pass out.

I had to hope the arsonist chose to continue running rather than sticking around to finish the job. I chuckled darkly to myself. I finally get the girl and now I might die alone in the woods. It was my own stupid fault. But all I saw was red when the fucker appeared at the tree line, like he was gloating over his latest success. Or taunting us.

Blood covered my hands when I pulled them away. That

wasn't good, and I knew I needed to keep the pressure steady, but I also needed to assess the wound. It didn't feel like the bullet penetrated, but I'd never been shot before, so I had no idea what that felt like.

I lifted my shirt, feeling around and scrutinizing the area. A long sigh slipped through my lips. It was just a graze. Still, I would need to get it cleaned and bandaged. I took in another deep breath and applied pressure to the wound.

After making sure the arsonist wasn't in sight, I got to my feet and started limping slowly back the way I came. Fatigue spread through my body within minutes, and I questioned if I could make it.

Fear enveloped me as movement through the trees caught my eye. Had the fucker hung around waiting to see what I would do? But my panic quickly morphed into relief as Dylan came into focus.

He glanced down to where I held my bloody side, and his jaw visibly clenched as his gaze bore into me. I could only hope he thought to bring a med kit. He shifted to the side and my heart took off running at the sight behind him.

My love.

"Oh my God," Lyla exclaimed, running toward me. She set the large jump bag down, and with shaky hands, tried to pull my shirt up.

I grasped her hands, stilling her movements. "Look at me, love."

Her head rose, meeting my eyes. Fear swam in the depths of hers.

"I'm okay. It's just a graze," I murmured.

Her shoulders relaxed and I pulled her against my body. She wrapped her arms around me and I couldn't stop the flinch of pain.

With a huff, she pulled away. "Let me see it."

I sighed, knowing there was no use arguing with her. Besides, it did need to be cleaned and bandaged, although I was pretty sure it needed stitches, which meant an ER visit.

"Did you get a good look at him?" Dylan crossed his arms over his chest.

I gritted my teeth and shook my head. "The minute I gained distance and got close, the fucker tried to shoot me."

He glared at me. "Apparently you missed the part where I said don't be a hero, and he did, in fact, shoot you."

I opened my mouth to make some dickhead remark, but slammed my teeth together and swallowed down a hiss as Lyla cleaned the wound on my side. I glanced down at her, taking in the look on her face that said she too wasn't happy about my moment of heroism—or rather, impulsive stupidity.

"Sorry," I breathed out, mostly directed at her and not Dylan.

She tended to me while Dylan and the officers he had with him continued on, leaving one to walk back with us. Once we cleared the tree line, Zack and the guys spotted us and came running.

"I'm fine." I waved them off as they tried to disentangle me from Lyla to help me walk to the rig. God, I hated to be fussed over. And if I had anyone's arm wrapped around me, I wanted it to be Lyla's.

I flinched as Zack crossed his arms, shooting me a glare, assuming he was also pissed at my stunt.

"I'm okay." I kept my gaze on Zack. "It's just a superficial graze."

A huff of annoyance came from Lyla. "Not the point. It could have been so much worse. And it's still bleeding and needs stitches. Nothing superficial about it. Not to mention the risk of infection." Her gaze bounced around the group, landing on Jay, who had recently gotten his EMT certification. "Can you drive the rig?"

Owen wanted all of the paid personnel certified before the end of the year. That way we could be an integrated fire/EMS station. Fortunately, Logan and Jay had finished theirs up a month ago, while Zack and Seth were still working on theirs.

Jay nodded. "Yeah, let me run it by the Lieutenant. We got the fire out so we should be good."

Lyla led me to the back of the ambo, sitting me down and pulling me against her. Wrapping me in her embrace, the pain and everything around us seemed to disappear. Her touch not only calmed my body, but my soul as well.

Instinctively, I knew. Everything would be okay.

Chapter Thirty-Eight

LYLA

I SLAMMED my hands on my hips and glared at Adam. He was the worst patient. A mix of stubborn and demanding. If he wasn't telling me he didn't need my help, he was telling me how to help him. I couldn't help but wonder if Violet was having similar issues with Seth who was also out of work recovering.

On top of being homebound and healing, he was still frustrated because they never found the arsonist—only the place in the woods where he'd been hiding out. They weren't able to pull prints off anything, but they did find a rusty old fire department button. Similar to ones we would give out at carnivals and fairs. It was for the station that the kids' godfather worked out of.

So even though it felt like a substantial piece of evidence, without DNA, it felt like we were all back to square one yet again.

It wasn't actually a total loss, though. Some of the puzzle pieces had started to fall together, and it all made sense. He hadn't been spotted getting to and from the houses because they all backed up to the large area of forest that weaved through and behind our town.

I pulled a calming breath into my lungs and softened my glare. "That was not what the doctor said."

He shrugged. "Pretty much. He said I can continue all normal activity as long as I feel up to it." His lips lifted into that sexy smirk of his. "And trust me, I definitely feel up to it."

I rolled my eyes. He was heading back to work later this week, and honestly, I was looking forward to it. The graze wasn't too bad, but the wound needed to fully close and be mostly healed before he could go back on shift. More than a week off, and with restrictions, had him going stir crazy. In more ways than one.

He took a step toward me, and I took one back, shaking my head. "You literally just got the stitches removed." I took another step back and hit the wall behind me.

He caged me in with his hands on either side of my head. "Lyla, my love." He cupped my face, brushing his thumb along my lower lip. Heat pooled low in my belly, and between his words and his touch, I didn't stand a chance. "I promise I'll take it easy. In fact, if it makes you happy, I'll let you do all the work. But I cannot wait another minute to be inside you. I need to feel you."

Before I could protest again, his mouth descended on mine. I melted into the kiss, my body coming alive, craving everything he was offering. I moaned into his mouth while his tongue explored every inch.

He trailed his mouth along my jaw and nipped at the shell of my ear. "You want that too, don't you?"

I tried to squeeze my legs together to relieve the throbbing at the apex of my thighs, but his knee wedged between them, stopping me.

"You're already soaked for me, aren't you?" He ran his hand

up my leg and under my sweater dress, brushing his fingers over the fabric of my lacy thong. "You were hoping I would be cleared and find out what you were wearing under this dress."

It wasn't a question. It was a statement. One I couldn't totally argue with.

But the doctor said he still wanted him to take it easy for the next day, and I didn't think that meant plowing into me until I saw stars.

The way his fingers dipped under the fabric, teasing and exploring, I was a writhing mess in seconds, completely forgetting about his injury and the doctor's orders.

"Tell me, love." He sucked on the sensitive skin of my neck, and I all but lost it. "Tell me you're as desperate as I am."

"I am. So desperate."

He pulled back, looking down at me, and removed his hand. His pupils blew out as he brought his fingers to his mouth, sucking my wetness off them and moaning like a starving man who'd just had his first bite of food.

I sighed. "I just don't want to hurt you."

He cupped my face with both of his hands and his gaze bore into me. "Nothing you will ever do could hurt me." He pressed his lips to my forehead. "Being with you will always bring me happiness, never pain."

I smiled, thinking how grumpy he'd been with me just a few days earlier when I demanded he sit down and let me take care of him. Even then, he had a very different, and probably better—or at least more fun—idea of what that entailed.

He searched my face. "Do you trust me?"

"With my whole heart," I whispered, running my hands up his chest and latching them behind his neck.

A smile lit up his face, like that was all he needed to know. He stepped back and grabbed my hand, pulling me down the hallway to our bedroom.

Concern and my own stubbornness gave way to anticipation,

and love and utter happiness swelled in my chest. I couldn't wait to spend forever with the insanely stubborn man who never failed to make me feel absolutely cherished and adored.

Epilogue

ADAM

I LEANED BACK and placed my arm around Lyla, pulling her close. Steam from the hot tub surrounded us and made it the perfect late-night activity. Too bad we weren't alone. Other guests from The Lodge milled about the pool area. I couldn't be mad, but that didn't stop me from considering pulling the fire alarm so they'd all clear out.

My love surprised me with the weekend trip for my thirtieth birthday. Walking through the lobby earlier, I couldn't stop picturing having our wedding there. She'd mentioned she thought it would be a great wedding venue. I smiled thinking about how her cheeks had flushed adorably as she'd stumbled over her words, attempting to clarify she meant in general, not for anyone in particular.

AJ RANNEY

God, I hoped that was a lie. That it was us she thought of. Getting married was never something I'd ever considered, but Lyla as my wife made perfect sense.

First, I needed a ring.

"Has Zack found another player for the volleyball game?"

I stiffened at the reminder of the large fire last month that took the life of one of our own. It still sat heavy in my gut. He would be honored at the annual PD vs. FD volleyball game coming up next week. But I didn't want either of us thinking about that right now and dampening our weekend.

"No, I don't think so." I smirked, pulling her closer to my side. "You sure you don't want to join the team?"

She raised a brow. "Do you want me to get another concussion?"

"Fair." I pressed my lips to her temple.

The water shifted as Zack stepped down into it. "Ahh... this feels good on my muscles after yesterday's shift."

I narrowed my eyes. "Thought you said you weren't gonna intrude on our romantic weekend."

He raised a brow. "Yeah, but that didn't mean I wasn't going to come use the pool and hot tub." He pointed at us. "You could have stayed in your room."

I huffed. He had a point, but Lyla wanted to swim and that was the only reason we were down here. We'd make good use of the tub in our room later.

"How's the lodge going with your parents away?"

"Fine. It pretty much runs itself. I tell them this every year when they stress about going on vacation." He looked over at Lyla. "You should have invited your friend Mia."

She laughed. "On our romantic weekend away?"

"Nah." He shook his head. "I just meant to come enjoy the pool and hot tub. Keep me company."

Her eyes widened. "She hates you."

"I'm pretty sure she hates everyone." He shrugged. "I'll grow

214

on her eventually. I always do. Once she realizes how easily I make her smile and laugh, she'll be putty in my hands."

He had that glint in his eye, and I sighed. It had become very clear over the years that he liked a challenge, but I really hoped he didn't have his eyes set on Mia. That was bound to blow up. Because I one hundred percent agreed with Lyla—Mia Carpenter actually hated Zack Stoer.

But what did I know? Stranger things had happened. Hell, six months ago I would never have believed this would be my life. That I would finally find my forever. I glanced down at Lyla as I tucked her further into my side, love and joy squeezing my chest.

More By A J Ranney

Half Moon Lake Series:
Always Yours (book 1)
Wishing to be Yours (book 1.5)
Impossibly Yours (book 2)
Imperfectly Yours (book 3)
Bravely Yours (book 3.5)
Recklessly Yours (book 4)

Half Moon Lake Heroes: The Red Line
Bravely Yours (book 0.5)
Playing with Fire
Out of the Fire
The Line of Fire
Calling a Cease Fire

WRITING AS GRACIE YORK
Goldilocks and the Grumpy Bear
Tumbling Head Over Heels
Along Came The Girl
Peter Pumpkined Out
Back Together Again
Ghost Shoes

Follow Me

Come be apart of my Facebook Group.
AJ's Book Nook

Find me on social media:
Instagram.com/a.j.ranney
Facebook.com/ajranney19
tiktok.com/@ajranney3
Goodreads.com/AJ Ranney
http://www.ajranney.com

Note from the Author

Dear Reader,

THANK YOU for reading *The Line of Fire*. Adam and Lyla were a bit of a challenge. That perfect balance of will they or won't they has to be perfect and I hope I got it right!

Next I'm working on Zack's story! Can you guess who the FMC will be!?

I appreciate each and every one of you. It's only because people like you read our books that authors like me get to publish them.

Check out my website for bonus content and stay up to date with latest releases.

Love,
AJ Ranney
www.ajranney.com

Acknowledgments

Like always, I need to thank my husband first. He has been one of my biggest cheerleaders, is always willing to listen to what I write, and has done bedtime with the kids more times than I probably realize. I appreciate your eagerness to help me when I'm stuck and your willingness to let me read to you.

And then to my kids, who are always curious about what Mommy is writing. And yes, you still need to wait until you're eighteen to read them. But by then I doubt you'd want to!

Jenn, I know you're sick of my stories by the time we get to this part! Regardless, thank you for dealing with my constant *how do I fix this?* questions and talking me down every time I'm ready to burn everything I write. You're always willing to read and edit multiple times, hold my hand when I need it, and tell me to just do it when I need that too. But above everything you've done, your friendship has meant the world to me.

A HUGE thank you to my author friends who have supported me in so many ways, whether through encouragement or reading my stuff: Annie Charme, Kat Long, Jenni Bara, Brittanee Nicole, Daphne Elliot, Kristin Lee, Amanda Zook, Alexandra Hale and many more!

Also to all my beta readers: thank you for always willing to read and give feedback!

Cami, thank you for all the graphics, reading and helping find teaser lines and the phone calls to chat and get organized. I appreciate all your help!

Michelle, a HUGE thank you goes out to you. Every

comment you left that made me stop and think, even when I wanted to push back. Your guidance really helped shape and mold this book. Thank you for always willing to answer questions or help me talk something out!

Holly, as always, thank you for being my sister, even if not by blood—and to my mom and mother-in-law: You have been so supportive throughout every step of this crazy journey!

And finally, thank you to the rest of my friends and family who have helped or supported me. I used to think it took a village to raise little humans, and that still holds true, but it also takes a village to write and publish a book!

About the Author

A.J. Ranney lives in Maryland with her ever-growing zoo, including two kids, two cats, an attention-loving dog, a bunny, a cricket-eating lizard, and her lovable, well-meaning husband. She likes to leave the chaos of her real world behind and lose herself in a steamy romance novel. Her passion for reading romance prompted her writing journey, leading her to create relatable happily ever afters that come from her own dreams and experiences.

She loves coffee, sushi, wine, and her family. Not necessarily in that order. Her inner peace comes from the water, always relating to her zodiac sign, the Pisces. It's no wonder the small town she created in her stories is situated on a lake.

www.ingramcontent.com/pod-product-compliance
Lightning Source LLC
Chambersburg PA
CBHW022140240626
47153CB00007B/2436